W9-AAG-066

"All aboard!" Freddie shouted

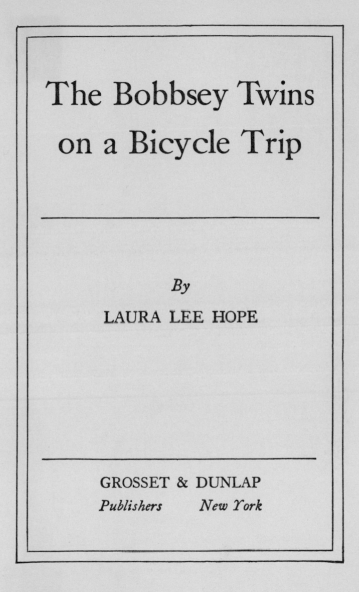

The Bobbsey Twins
on a Bicycle Trip

By

LAURA LEE HOPE

GROSSET & DUNLAP
Publishers   *New York*

© Grosset & Dunlap, Inc. 1958

ISBN: 0-448-08048-6

Copyright, 1954, by
Grosset & Dunlap, Inc.
All Rights Reserved

—————

Printed in the United States of America

The Bobbsey Twins on a Bicycle Trip

CONTENTS

CONTENTS

CHAPTER I

SNOWBALL DISAPPEARS

"WE'RE home!" shrieked Flossie Bobbsey.

The plump blond girl of six jumped from the car. Her twin brother Freddie, who looked very much like Flossie and also had big blue eyes, scrambled after her. They were followed by Nan and Bert, who were twelve years old. Nan and Bert were twins, too, but did not look like their small brother and sister. They had dark hair and eyes.

"But it was fun at Uncle Daniel's farm," Nan said.

"Sure it was," said Freddie, "but they didn't have one single fire engine for me to play with."

Everyone laughed, including tall, good-looking Mr. Bobbsey and Mrs. Bobbsey, who was seated alongside him. She was very pretty, with sparkling eyes and a cheerful smile.

Bert began to take the luggage from the car. Flossie waited until he had removed two big bags, then she climbed into the back seat. As she leaned over, Bert noticed a basket covered with a shawl.

"What's in there?" he asked.

"A secret," Flossie whispered. "Don't tell anybody."

The little girl removed the shawl and opened the lid of the basket. Then she gave a little scream, and the others turned to see what had happened.

"She's gone!" Flossie cried.

"Who's gone?" Mrs. Bobbsey asked quickly.

"Snowball! My darling pussycat Snowball!" the little girl replied. The pure white kitten had been given to her the year before by Uncle Daniel as a playmate for their older cat, Snoop.

The little girl burst out crying, jumped from the car, and buried her head in her mother's skirt.

"Flossie!" Mrs. Bobbsey said, stroking her small daughter's curls. "You mean you brought Snowball back home with you—and she's gone?"

"Ye—ye—yes," Flossie sobbed. She knew she should have left the cat at Uncle Daniel's farm, but at the last minute she couldn't bear to leave Snowball behind. Uncle Daniel needed a good mouser, which Snowball was, and so she was to have stayed at the farm a couple of months.

"She's gone!" Flossie cried

"And now she's lost! Oh, Mother, what shall we do?"

No one knew exactly what to do. Each of them asked Flossie when she had last seen Snowball. She told them that when they had stopped for luncheon at a restaurant, she had given Snowball an airing and then put her back in the basket. The family tried to figure out how many times they had stopped along the route. Once Mr. Bobbsey had checked the tires. Another time Nan had wanted to pick some wild flowers.

"And we stopped once to buy gas," Bert said.

It was decided that Snowball might have escaped at any one of these points.

"Why don't we drive back and find her?" Freddie suggested.

Mr. Bobbsey said it was a long way and it was doubtful the cat had remained near the road. But to please Flossie, he said he would go part way back.

The car was completely unloaded and Mrs. Bobbsey said that she would remain at the house. The children's father took the four twins with him and retraced their route. It was decided that Freddie and Bert would watch out of one side of the car while Nan and Flossie would watch out of the other. After they had driven for some time, Flossie sighed.

"I don't see anything but dogs," she said. "Do you suppose these are all lost dogs?"

Her father said he thought not. Dogs loved to roam long distances but always found their way home.

"As a matter of fact," he said, "cats find their way home too."

This made Flossie feel better, but she decided nevertheless that they should go on and see if they could find her beloved cat. They rode several miles farther without seeing any animals except cows grazing in the fields, when suddenly Freddie cried out, "I see Snowball!"

It seemed as if Freddie might be right. They had come to a little woods, and off in the distance they could see a cat running along. Mr. Bobbsey stopped the car and Freddie and Flossie jumped out. The little boy scooted up the embankment and into the woods.

"Snowball!" he shouted.

The cat he had seen did not stop at once, but the little boy kept on running. Suddenly the animal disappeared among some brush. Freddie ran up to the spot and reached his hand down among the branches. The next second he gave a loud scream.

The cat had scratched him badly!

"Oh!" Freddie cried. "You're not Snowball at all!"

Hearing the boy scream, the other Bobbseys came running up. They were just in time to see the cat flash out of the brush and run deeper into the woods. Freddie was right, it was not Snowball.

Mr. Bobbsey bound a clean handkerchief around Freddie's bleeding hand. He decided they had looked long enough for Snowball and said they should go back. Flossie was disappointed, for she felt sure they would have to make a more thorough search in order to find the cat.

Bert put his arm around his little sister and said, "I'll tell you what. Let's put an ad in the paper. Maybe somebody has found Snowball."

Flossie liked this idea and asked if they could possibly get it into the next morning's paper. Mr. Bobbsey said they would stop at the newspaper office and try. Upon reaching it, Bert hopped out and went in. Soon he returned, saying they were not too late, and Flossie clapped her hands gleefully.

When they arrived home, the twins were greeted by the elderly colored couple who had worked for the Bobbsey family for many years. Stout, good-natured Dinah cooked for the family, while her husband Sam, who had the whitest teeth the children had ever seen, drove a truck in Mr. Bobbsey's lumber business.

"I'm sure sorry to hear about Snowball," said Dinah. "But don't forget, cats take powerful good care o' themselves. Now don't you-all worry about her."

"That's right," Sam added. "Cats are certainly smart. Why, I once knew a cat that took six months to get back home, but she did it!"

Nan smiled at the couple. Ever since she could remember, Dinah and Sam had been around, doing kind things for the children. And always making them feel better when they were in trouble.

Dinah had prepared a delicious supper, and the family sat down at once to eat. Even before the meal ended, Flossie and Freddie began to yawn and were glad to go to bed right after dessert. Freddie shared a room with Bert, and Flossie slept in a twin bed in Nan's room.

All the twins awoke early and rushed downstairs in bathrobes and slippers to look at the morning paper. Quickly Bert turned to the classified ad section and pointed to the ad asking for information about a missing cat named Snowball.

"Do you suppose we'll get any answers?" Flossie asked excitedly.

She had hardly finished speaking when the telephone rang. Nan, who was standing nearest it, answered.

"No," the others heard her say. "Our cat wasn't yellow and black striped. But thank you for calling."

Bert grinned. "I should have put in the ad that Snowball is pure white."

"Let's eat breakfast right now," Freddie proposed. "I'm hungry."

The children trooped into the kitchen and found Dinah already there. She said the orange juice was ready and the oatmeal cooked. It would not take long to make toast. The children could sit down at the dining room table at once. They had just taken their places when the phone rang again. Bert dashed to answer it. The others listened eagerly.

"I'm sorry," they heard him say, laughing. "But Snowball's a lady cat. She's not a tom cat."

The other children giggled. There were two other calls, both of them from people who wanted to give cats away.

Flossie sighed. "Oh dear," she said, "we're not having any luck at all."

"Don't be discouraged," Nan comforted her. "The phone calls have only just begun!"

The children got dressed and then took turns sitting near the telephone. When it was Nan's turn, Flossie and Freddie went out in the back yard to play. Freddie had just dragged his pumper engine out of the garage when a boy about Bert's age hopped the hedge.

"Hello, kids!" he said.

"Hello, Danny," the twins replied. They did not care for Danny Rugg. He was always causing them trouble and was known around Lakeport as a young bully.

But just now they forgot their dislike of the boy, because he said, "I know where your old cat is!"

"You do?" the children cried. "Where?"

"Oh, a little ways from here in the woods," Danny said. "I saw her there a little while ago."

"Please, *please* show us!" Flossie begged.

"Okay," Danny said, moving off. "Follow me." Then, looking back over his shoulder at the twins, he added, "Snowball was so high up in a tree, I don't think she's ever coming down!"

CHAPTER II

A RESCUE

WHEN Flossie heard that her lovely cat
Snowball might never get down out of the tree
she was very sad. But suddenly Freddie had
an idea. He remembered having seen a cat res-
cued from a telephone pole the year before.

All the Bobbsey twins, though young, were
full of ideas. This fact had brought many
adventures to them—some very pleasant and
others quite alarming. They had been on several vacations with their parents and each time
had come across an exciting mystery. Recently,
the twins had helped solve a puzzling one at
Big Bear Pond.

"We can get the fire department to bring
Snowball down," Freddie told Flossie and
Danny Rugg.

"That's right," said Flossie hopefully. "As
soon as we see which tree Snowball's in, we'll
run home and call the fire department."

By this time the three children were a good
distance from the Bobbsey house. When they

were about a mile from their home, Danny
turned off into a woods.

"Oh, I know where this is," said Flossie. "See
that big tree over there with the hole in it?
I remember that when we were driving home."

Excited now at the hope that Danny really
had seen Snowball in a tree, the twins hurried
after him. He went deeper and deeper into the
woods. Finally he stopped and looked up. "It
was this tree, I think," he said.

The two little children looked up eagerly.
Their eyes roamed from branch to branch, but
they did not see Snowball. Finally both of them
began to call their cat. There was no answering
meow.

"Maybe she moved to another tree," said
Freddie.

The twins looked toward one close by. They
stood on tiptoe, peered up at each bough, and
again called. But the cat did not appear.

"Oh dear," said Flossie. "Danny, are you
sure you saw Snowball here?"

As she spoke, the little girl looked around
for Danny Rugg. The boy was not in sight.

"Danny, where are you?" she called. The
older boy did not reply.

"You're mean!" Flossie said. "This is serious. We don't want to play hide-and-seek now
. . . we want to find Snowball."

Still Danny did not appear. Freddie became angry and called to the big boy that it was no fair to have led them here and then start to play games. There was no response from the other boy.

The small twins decided to ignore him and began walking around, looking up into all the trees. From time to time they would call Snowball's name. But their missing cat apparently was not in any of the trees.

"Okay, Danny," Freddie called out. "I guess Snowball's gone. We'd better go home."

The small twins waited a couple of minutes for Danny to come back. When he still did not show up, Freddie and Flossie finally realized the bully had played another mean trick on them. He had deliberately led them into the woods and gone off without them. They began to doubt that he had even seen Snowball.

"Danny's the meanest boy in all Lakeport!" Flossie cried, stamping her foot.

"I'll say!" Freddie agreed. "Well, I guess we'd better go home."

He started off ahead of his twin. They walked in silence for some time, jumping over fallen logs. There was no path, and Freddie had no direction marks to follow. After they had walked for some time, Flossie called out:

"Freddie, let's sit down. I'm terrible tired."

The two children flopped onto the ground and looked around them. Flossie remarked that she did not remember any part of the woods that looked like this when they had entered it. Freddie admitted that he did not either.

"Maybe we ought to go the other way," he said. "But first let's find something to eat. I'm awful hungry."

The children looked around them for some sign of a familiar bush. At first they did not see any. Then Freddie spied some huckleberry bushes. They picked some fruit and began eating it. The berries were sweet and tasty, but in a moment Freddie said:

"I wish we were home, eating some of Dinah's cookies."

"I do too," said Flossie. "Well, let's go now."

The twins decided that Flossie would be the leader this time. She thought she recognized a little brook which they had crossed when Danny brought them into the woods. But after they had gone over this landmark and walked for some time, the little girl stopped.

"We're not coming to the road at all," she said.

The children wondered what to do next. Flossie was trying hard not to be frightened, but she wondered what might happen if she and Freddie had to stay in the woods all day and all night.

Suddenly the little girl thought she heard a dog barking. "Listen!" she said.

Both children could hear it now. The barking was getting louder. Flossie grabbed her twin's hand.

"Freddie," she cried excitedly. "That sounds just like our Waggo!"

"It sure does!" Freddie exclaimed and started to run in the direction of the barking.

Presently a little fox terrier crashed through the underbrush. It was Waggo indeed! Joyfully he bounded up to them and began to lick their hands.

"Oh, Waggo, you old darling!" cried Flossie. "You found us!"

The dog jumped around gleefully for a few moments, then started back through the woods. The children skipped after him. It was hard to keep up to Waggo. Each time he got out of sight, they called him to come back and the fox terrier obeyed.

The long walk back to the road made Flossie and Freddie realize how far they had wandered from the spot where Danny had left them. They were angrier than ever with the boy, and Freddie declared he was going to fight the big boy.

"I don't care if he is taller than I am," he said. "He can't do things like this to us!"

When they reached the road, Waggo bounded ahead of them, starting to bark all over again.

"He's like a messenger telling everybody we're safe," Flossie said, giggling.

The twins had gone only two blocks when they saw Nan and Bert hurrying toward them. The older twins hugged their brother and sister and Nan said, "Oh, we've been so worried about you. What happened?"

Freddie told the story and Bert's face darkened. He said it would not be necessary for Freddie to go fight Danny. Bert would be glad to do it himself.

"That's one of the meanest tricks a person can play," he said. "Leaving anyone stranded in the forest."

Flossie asked whether they had sent Waggo out to hunt for them. Nan said no. Then suddenly she remembered that Danny had come back to the house. She had seen the bully talking to Waggo.

"Maybe he sent Waggo after you," she suggested.

Bert went off to find out. He walked straight to Danny's home and into the back yard. He spotted the boy in the garage.

Danny saw him at the same moment and came outside.

"What are you doing here?" he asked.

"I guess you know," said Bert, doubling his fists.

"So you want to fight, eh?" said Danny jeeringly. "It's okay with me."

"Nobody can leave my little brother and sister in the woods and get away with it!" Bert retorted, his eyes flashing.

"Aw, you'd think Freddie and Flossie were sissies. They're not as big sissies as you are. Anyhow, I sent your dog Waggo to find them."

"You didn't know for sure Waggo would find them," Bert said.

He lashed out at the bully, giving him a hard punch in the chest. Danny came back with a sharp thrust at Bert's jaw. The boy dodged just in time. The fight had gone only this far when a voice called:

"Boys, stop that fighting at once!"

Bert and Danny turned to see Mrs. Rugg hurrying toward them. She wanted to know what it was all about. Both boys remained silent.

"Well, I guess if you won't tell me, it isn't too serious. Bert Bobbsey, go home at once and don't come around here again starting fights for nothing!"

Not being a tattletale, Bert obeyed her command. As he moved off, he saw a sneer come over Danny's face and this infuriated him.

Bert was walking along the street with his head down, thinking, when another boy's voice called, "Hey, Bert, what's eating you?"

The Bobbsey twin looked up to see his friend, Charlie Mason, smiling at him.

"Hi, Charlie!" he said, and then told the boy what had happened. Charlie agreed that leaving Freddie and Flossie lost in the woods was a mean stunt indeed.

"That sounds just like Danny," Charlie said. "And let me tell you something else about him. Bert, do you want to help me solve a mystery?"

CHAPTER III

A LOST BUGLE

THERE was nothing Bert Bobbsey liked better than to solve a mystery. At once, he asked Charlie Mason to explain how he might help his friend.

"While you and your family were away visiting your uncle Daniel," Charlie began, "my dad took me and a bunch of fellows on a camping trip. We went to Beechcroft Hill. Know where it is?"

"I remember seeing it when we were coming home from Uncle Daniel's," Bert replied. "It's about fifteen or twenty miles from here, isn't it?"

Charlie said that it was. He had heard that the owners were going to sell the place off for building lots. "I don't know much about it. My dad got permission for us to camp there. I think an aunt of mine was going to buy the property and Dad wanted to look it over for her."

Charlie went on, "You remember the

neat gold-plated bugle I won at the contest?"

Bert Bobbsey remembered it very well. There had been a contest among all the school children of Lakeport who played musical instruments. Charlie played the bugle very well and had won the contest, receiving the fine instrument as a prize for his outstanding performance.

"I took my bugle along to get the fellows up in the morning," Charlie explained. "But the last night we were there it disappeared."

"You mean it was taken by someone?" Bert asked.

Charlie said that at first he had thought one of the other fellows had played a trick on him, but when the bugle could not be found they insisted they knew nothing about it.

"So we're pretty sure it must have been stolen," Charlie said.

"Boy, that's a shame," said Bert sympathetically. "And is that the mystery you want me to help you solve?"

His friend nodded. He said that he and his father had inquired in the second-hand shops and stores where musical instruments were sold. But his prize bugle had not been turned in.

"Do you have any clues at all?" Bert asked him.

"Well, no regular ones," Charlie answered. "But I have kind of a hunch myself. My dad doesn't want me to accuse anybody unjustly, so I haven't said a word about it. But I can tell you, Bert, and see what you think."

Charlie said that one day while walking in the woods near their camp site he had seen another group of boys. They had not been close enough for him to identify them all, but one certainly looked very much like Danny Rugg.

"You mean they were camping there?" Bert wanted to know.

"I don't know whether they were staying all night or not," Charlie replied. "When I saw the boys they were moving off. I called Danny, and they all started to run. They were too far away for me to catch up, so I let them go."

Bert was thoughtful. If Danny Rugg was with the group of boys, then very possibly he had taken Charlie's bugle for a joke. When he thought that Charlie had worried long enough, maybe he would return the instrument. But how long this might be was the question.

"Well, what do you think?" Charlie asked Bert.

"We'll have to find out," Bert said, "whether or not Danny has the bugle. But first, we'd better make sure he was in the woods then."

"You're right," said Charlie.

The boys decided that the easiest way to determine this was to approach one of Danny's pals, Jack Westley. He probably would have been with him on any camping trip.

Accordingly they went over to the Westley home. Jack, who was also about Bert's and Charlie's age, was Danny's best friend. Seeing him on his front porch steps, the two boys acted as if they were just passing by and, waving to Jack, walked beyond the house. Then, as if they wished to be friendly, Bert and Charlie turned back.

"Did you have fun on your camping trip?" Bert asked. "I've been away myself and just heard about it."

He and Charlie almost laughed out loud, but they managed to keep straight faces. Jack fell into their trap at once.

"Sure, I had a swell time," he replied. "Those hills make a good camping spot."

"Yes," said Charlie, "but we won't be allowed to go there after they sell the place."

"I suppose not," said Jack.

Bert and Charlie strolled on and it was not until they had turned the corner, out of sight of Jack, that the two of them burst out laughing. Charlie slapped Bert on the shoulder and said:

"You're a swell detective. We're going to

solve the case of the missing bugle in no time at all."

"The next part'll be harder," said Bert. "Finding out if Danny has the bugle."

Charlie asked his friend if he had any suggestions and Bert thought hard as they walked along. It was not until they stopped in a drugstore and had a soda that he came up with an idea.

"You know, Charlie," he said, "my father's bookkeeper, Mr. Jones, lives over at Columbus. His son Bill leads a little band. I'm sure I could get him to help us out."

Charlie asked how he intended to do this. Bert explained that if Bill Jones would go along with them, he thought they surely could find out if Danny had the bugle.

"Bill could call Danny on the phone and tell him he has something to show him," Bert explained. "Bill would bring over his band and play for Danny. After a while he'd ask him if he has an instrument and would like to join."

Charlie burst out laughing. "That's a swell plan, Bert. I think Danny can play the bugle a little and he'll be sure to bring out mine if he has it."

The boys went to the telephone booth. Bert put in a call to Bill Jones in Columbus and found him at home. After hearing the plan, Bill readily agreed.

"I've heard about Danny and his mean ways,' he said. "I'll be glad to show him up."

Bert gave Bill Danny's telephone number and then asked Bill to let him know if he succeeded in making a date with the boy.

That afternoon a phone call came to the Bobbsey house for Bert. He was delighted to learn that Danny was very eager to see what Bill had to show him.

"I'm bringing my band over on the bus tomorrow morning," said Bill.

"I'll meet you," Bert offered, "and go with you to Danny's house. Then Charlie and I will hide and see what happens."

As Bert finished talking to Bill, Nan came down the stairs. Immediately her brother confided the whole plan to her. Nan said she hoped it would prove whether or not Danny had Charlie's bugle.

A few moments later Nan said to her twin, "Maybe it was over at Beechcroft Hill that Danny saw Snowball. It might have put the idea in his head to play a joke on Flossie and Freddie."

"I'll bet he did," replied Bert. "What say we go over to Beechcroft Hill and take a look?"

The two children rushed upstairs to ask permission of Mrs. Bobbsey. She said that if the twins would promise not to go too deep into the woods, they might go and look for the missing cat and the bugle.

"Take a number ten bus from the center of Lakeport," she said, going for her purse to give them some money. "They only run every half hour, so be sure to find out when you can catch one coming back so you'll be home before suppertime."

Bert, Nan, and Mrs. Bobbsey decided to say nothing about the trip to the smaller twins. Flossie and Freddie had been disappointed so many times already that it seemed best not to tell them unless Bert and Nan should bring the cat back with them. Excitedly they started off, running almost the whole way to downtown Lakeport.

"There's a number ten bus," Nan cried.

The two ran as fast as they could and just made the bus. Settling back in their seats, the twins relaxed for a while without talking. The bus proved to be an express and it was not long before the driver was calling out:

"Next stop, Beechcroft Hill."

The twins alighted and immediately set off into the woods. Each one was looking for a spot where Snowball might have been likely to stay.

They paused at a little cave and peeked into
a hollow tree. After a while they began to call:
"Snowball! Are you here?"

Their missing pet did not come, but suddenly there appeared from behind a clump of

bushes a very thin, bony-looking man with thin
gray hair. On his head was a three-cornered
green velvet hat. In one hand he carried a long
whip.

"Get out of here!" he shouted angrily at the
children. "Get out!"

CHAPTER IV

AS THE strange man came hurrying toward Bert and Nan, waving his whip, the children retreated.

"Get out of here! As fast as you can!" he shouted again. "And don't ever come back!"

Suddenly Nan's heel caught in a tree root and she lost her balance. Down she went on a bed of pine needles. Bert stooped to help her up, giving the old fellow a chance to come closer.

"We'd better run!" urged Nan, eying the whip fearfully.

But this time Bert stood his ground and called, "Do you own these woods?"

"That's none of your business!" was the angry reply.

"I think it is," Bert insisted. "If you don't own them, you have no right to order us away."

The boy's statement evidently surprised the old man. He suddenly stopped running and lowered his whip. He admitted he did not own the woods, but he was caretaker for the man whose property it was.

"You're a pretty smart boy," he said. "What do you want here?"

Bert explained that they were looking for their missing cat. As soon as they had searched the place thoroughly, they would leave.

"Perhaps you saw our Snowball?" Nan asked, smiling at the man, who no longer looked frightening. "She's pure white."

"No, I haven't seen your cat," the caretaker answered. "I'll let you look around a little while, but I'm goin' to stay right with you. There's been too many pesky kids around these woods lately, and I aim to keep 'em out of here."

He asked what the children's names were, and, upon hearing them, said that he was Jed Rustum. He seemed almost friendly now, and helped the children look among the trees and call Snowball's name. But she did not appear, and finally the children said they must catch the bus and go home.

"Isn't this land for sale?" Nan asked.

"Yes, 'tis," Jed Rustum said. "But it's not to my likin' and it wouldn't have been to the old gentleman who owned this place originally. He's got a son here now who doesn't care anything about the property. He's sellin' it off in buildin' lots. He's gonna ruin it!"

The children made no comment on this, but Bert spoke about the various campers who had been there. Surely they had had permission from the owner. His remark set the old man off again. He waved his arms angrily, saying:

"Permission? They never got any permission far as I know. I was laid up sick a couple of weeks. Guess they must have helped themselves to the place while I was away."

The twins smiled. It was possible Danny Rugg had helped himself to the place, but certainly Charlie Mason's father never would have done such a thing.

"A friend of ours lost a bugle in these woods," Nan said. "You don't mind if we look around for it, do you, Mr. Rustum?"

Grudgingly, the old man said to go ahead, but added, "I thought you had to go home."

"Oh, we do," said Nan. "I just meant, instead of taking a straight line back to the bus we might zigzag around and see if our cat's here or if the bugle's lying on the ground anywhere."

Jed Rustum followed the children all the way to the main road. Upon reaching it, without having seen anything of Charlie's lost instrument, Bert said to the caretaker, "The bugle's a fine one—gold-plated and very valuable. If you see it, would you please save it for us?"

If Bert had suddenly tackled Mr. Rustum, he could not have produced a stronger reaction than came over the old man. He waved his arms around wildly, and shouted:

"Save it? If I find that bugle, I'm gonna smash it to bits!"

Nan and Bert looked at each other.

The old man calmed down a little. "I guess you think I'm batty," he said. "Well, I'm not. I just hate bugle calls. It reminds me of my days in the Army when I had to get up at the crack of dawn. To this day, bugle blowin' makes cold chills go up and down my spine."

Nan went up to the old man and laid a hand on his arm. She smiled at him, saying, "Mr. Rustum, if you find the bugle, you don't have to blow it. Just keep it and telephone us. We'll come and get it and promise not to make a sound on it."

Jed Rustum relaxed. The girl's remark seemed to tickle him, for he began to chuckle. He took a pad and pencil from his trouser pocket and handed it to Nan. "Here, write your phone number down. If I find that bugle, I'll give you a ring, and please keep off this property from now on." Nan did as he requested, then she and her twin said good-by and walked to the bus stop.

Meanwhile, there had been several more telephone calls at the Bobbsey home, but none of them brought any word of Snowball.

Finally Mrs. Bobbsey insisted that the small twins go out to the back yard and play. "Better see if your fire engine is working," she suggested to Freddie.

Ever since the little boy had been old enough to toddle, he had been greatly interested in fire engines. He had a toy fire engine and pumper which could really squirt water. Now he pulled the pumper from the garage and filled

it with water from a faucet at the side of the
house.

Off to one side of the garden, Flossie was
busy washing out some doll clothes in a small
tub. Freddie's eyes twinkled. He hitched up
the end of the hose to his pumper and turned the
nozzle, directing a stream of water into the
tub of clothes. But the force was greater than
he had thought.

*The next instant every single doll's garment
flew through the air!*

"Oh, Freddie!" Flossie cried. "Now I'll have
to wash them all over again!"

"I'm sorry," said Freddie. "I'll help you."

"No," replied Flossie. "You go play with your old pumper somewhere else."

Freddie shrugged, dragged the pumper away, and again searched the back yard for a place where he could spray the water and not do any damage. He decided on the side of the garage. He would pretend it was a house. He wheeled his pumper into position and got the hose ready. Gazing upward, he said to himself:

"This beautiful house is on fire! I must save it!"

As Freddie stared ahead of him, he could hardly believe his eyes. Smoke—real smoke—was coming through the open window! The garage *was* on fire!

CHAPTER V

THE SHOW-OFF

"FIRE! Fire!" Freddie yelled at the top of his lungs.

Flossie paid no attention, because she was quite used to Freddie's yelling when he was playing with any of his fire-fighting equipment. Dinah, in the kitchen, felt the same way and did not stop mixing the cake she was making for supper.

"Fire! It's a *real* fire! Help! Everybody come!" Freddie screamed.

This time Flossie looked up and saw the smoke curling from the garage window. Her eyes wide, she called out, "Dinah! Mother! The garage is on fire!"

Hearing this, Mrs. Bobbsey and the cook dashed from the house.

Suddenly Freddie realized this was his big chance to be what he had always wanted to be! Holding the hose steady in his two chubby hands, he turned the nozzle on full force and let the water spray through the open window of the garage. By the time his mother and Dinah reached the interior of the building, the smoke was gone. But the window sill was charred.

Mrs. Bobbsey made a quick investigation and guessed that the fire had been caused by a short circuit in the wiring system. There was a burned, oil-soaked rag on the window sill that evidently had been ignited.

When the excitement died down, Mrs. Bobbsey hugged her small son. "Freddie, you're a real fireman now!" she said.

Mrs. Bobbsey decided to have an electrician come up to see about the trouble. In the meantime she went to the cellar and turned off the main switch controlling the garage lights.

Flossie and Dinah added their praise, and when Mr. Bobbsey and, later, the older twins came home they were told the story and they patted the little fireman on the back.

Just before suppertime, an electrician arrived. Everyone hurried to the garage with him to hear the report. After an inspection, he said that Mrs. Bobbsey had been right.

"It was a short circuit all right," he explained, "caused by frayed wires." As the man quickly repaired the trouble, he added, "It was a good thing somebody saw that fire soon after it started. It could have burned the garage to the ground." This made Freddie feel even more elated.

During the evening there was little conversation about anything except the fire. Just before saying good night and going to their rooms, Bert remarked to Nan:

"Well, tomorrow we pull the stunt on Danny."

Nan wished her brother luck in finding out whether the bully had taken Charlie's prize bugle.

Next morning Bert left the house promptly at 9:30. On the way to the bus terminal he picked up Charlie Mason, and the two boys hurried along. In a few minutes the bus from Columbus pulled in.

Bill Jones was the first one off, followed by the other members of his band. Bert introduced Bill to Charlie, and all the other boys in turn were introduced to one another.

Bert led the way down a side street so that not too much attention would be directed to the band.

When they reached Danny's street, Bert and Charlie pointed out the Rugg home, and then darted down a driveway. Crossing several back yards, they came to the house next to Danny's. From here, without being seen, they could watch what was going on.

Presently Bert nudged his friend—Bill's band was assembling in the Ruggs' driveway. Soon they started to play. How the music shattered the stillness of the morning!

"Wowee!" Charlie exclaimed. "Those fellows sure can play!"

Bert agreed, but wished they would not play so loudly. All over the neighborhood people began poking their heads from windows and opening doors to see where the loud music was coming from. The six boys, directed by Bill, continued to play without interruption, swinging from one tune to another.

Danny Rugg, followed by his mother, had come out onto their front walk. They stared at the band players in amazement. Finally Mrs. Rugg called:

"What does this mean?"

When Bill Jones and his friends did not reply, Mrs. Rugg turned to Danny and asked if he knew anything about what was going on. Her son shook his head. Then he walked over to the group and said:

"Hey, what's the idea, fellows?"

Bill Jones waved for his group to stop playing. "Are you Danny Rugg?" he asked.

"Yes, I am. What's that got to do with it?"

"I'm Bill Jones," the visitor said.

Danny's jaw dropped. Then he stammered,

"You—you—you're the fellow who telephoned and said you had something to show me?"

The bandleader smiled and admitted that he was the one. "I wanted to show you how we play and see if you would like to join us."

"What do you mean?" Danny asked, puzzled.

"Don't you play an instrument?" Bill Jones asked him. "I heard that you did."

Danny looked surprised. He said that he played the bugle a little in school but did not own one.

"Don't you have one here at home?" Bill asked.

Danny shook his head. Bill pretended to be disappointed and asked if Danny had no musical instruments at all in the house. Suddenly the bully's face brightened. "Yes, I do have something," he said. "I'll bring it down."

He dashed into the house and returned a moment later with a harmonica. "I'm good at this," he bragged. The members of the band had a hard time keeping their faces straight. They had found out what Bert Bobbsey wanted to know—that Danny did not have Charlie's bugle. But it was his little harmonica compared to their large band instruments that struck them funny.

"Let's hear you play it," Bill suggested.

Danny needed no prompting. Putting the harmonica to his lips, the bully began. The resulting sounds were awful! Danny kept blowing wrong notes and finally, in a rage, he stopped and dashed into the house. His mother, frowning at the other boys, followed.

From a window Danny saw Bert and Charlie come out of hiding. They spied Danny watching them from behind the blind.

"Bet that show-off is burned up, all right," Charlie grinned. Then he added, "I wonder if he'll guess the real reason for the stunt."

"If he knows anything about your bugle, he'll guess," said Bert as the whole group moved off down the street. "But one thing's sure, it's not in the Rugg house. We'll have to look somewhere else for it."

The boys all had an early lunch in a downtown soda shop, then Bill and his six players took the bus back to Columbus. Bert and Charlie, walking together toward their homes, continued to discuss the missing bugle.

Suddenly Bert slapped Charlie on the back. He said he had an idea on how to look not only for the bugle but also for the Bobbseys' missing cat.

"What is it?" Charlie asked eagerly.

Bert said, "How about you and I going on a bicycle trip to look for them?"

CHAPTER VI

A BICYCLE PROBLEM

"SAY, Bert, that's a keen idea," said Charlie Mason. "Looking for my bugle and your cat might take several days. So we could make a bicycle camping trip out of it."

The two boys excitedly began to make plans. They could strap sleeping bags on their backs, and carry food in their bicycle baskets.

"I'll have to get a new poncho," said Bert. "Mine got a big hole in it up at Uncle Daniel's."

He told Charlie how he had been playing with a goat, pretending he was a matador.

"The goat was a bull I had to kill," Bert said. "But my old poncho that I was using for a cape wasn't strong enough, and when the goat's horns hit it they went right through!"

Charlie howled at the picture of Bert playing bullfighter with a goat, and asked what happened in the end. "Did you get the best of the goat?"

"No," Bert replied. "The goat butted me a

couple of times! Boy, real matadors must have to practice a lot to keep out of the way of maddened bulls."

As the two boys neared Charlie's home, Bert said suddenly, "Charlie, you and I have been making a lot of plans and we haven't even got permission yet to make the bicycle trip."

"You're right. But wait here a minute, Bert, and I'll go ask my mother."

Charlie went into the house, and came back a few minutes later to say that if Mr. and Mrs. Bobbsey would permit Bert to go, Charlie might accompany him.

"Gee, that's swell," said Bert. "I'll go ask my folks and call up to tell you what they say."

The Bobbsey twin hurried home. He found his mother upstairs sewing and immediately made his request. She said the idea sounded very good, but Bert would have to ask his father as well.

Bert flew to the telephone and called Mr. Bobbsey at his office. But Mr. Jones, the bookkeeper, said the boy's father was out and would not be back until five. So Bert had several hours to wait.

While Bert was talking, Flossie and Freddie had come into the hall. Overhearing a few words, they instantly wanted to know what their older brother had been talking about. When he

told them, the small twins shouted together:
"We want to go too!"

Bert was sure they were too young. He and Charlie would have a hard time managing them, and besides, they could not pedal fast enough.

"I'm afraid we can't take you," Bert said as kindly as he could.

"Why not?" Freddie demanded, "Last Christmas I got a two-wheeler and I can ride it fine now."

"Me too," Flossie spoke up. "Oh, Bert, you just have to take us! It will be a wonderful way to look for Snowball."

At this moment Nan came into the house through the kitchen. She asked what the discussion was about. Flossie told her the story.

Bert's twin laughed and looked at him. "Why, Bert," she said, "you wouldn't leave me out if everyone else is going, would you?"

Bert knew his twin was teasing him. "I won't know whether even I can go until Dad comes home," the older boy told the others.

He related the stunt he, Bill Jones, and Charlie had pulled on Danny Rugg. Flossie clapped her hands gleefully and said, "I'm glad you paid Danny back for leaving Freddie and me in the woods!"

The thought of the possible trip made all the

twins run out to the garage to check their bicycles. Bert and Nan had had theirs for years. Bert's had been new when purchased, but Nan's was second-hand. Now, gazing at it, she wondered if it would stand the long trip.

"I think I'll take my bike down to Smilin' Syd's shop," she said, "and have it serviced."

Smilin' Syd was a delightful man who was an expert at fixing bicycles. He had once told the twins that when he was a young man he had been in bicycle races. Bert loved to stop in and hear stories of how Syd had won many medals for being such a good rider.

At first Bert thought he would go with his sister. Then he remembered that he had promised his father to mow the grass. He would have to test his bicycle afterwards.

"See you later," he said to his twin.

On the way, Nan passed Nellie Parks' house. Nellie was her special friend. Suddenly it occurred to her that if the whole group did go on the bicycle trip, it would be fun to have a pal along.

"Bert will have Charlie," Nan told herself. "And Flossie and Freddie will be together. I think I'll stop and tell Nellie what's in the wind."

Her playmate was home, and the two girls sat out on the front lawn in the swing and discussed the possible trip. Nellie was a pretty, blue-eyed girl with long golden hair.

"Sounds wonderful," she said when Nan finished talking. "Oh, I do hope your dad will let all of you go and that my mother will give me permission!"

A sudden sad thought struck Nan. "I'm sure," she said, "that even if Daddy does allow Bert and Charlie to go on a bicycle trip alone, he'd never let us girls and Freddie and Flossie go."

Nellie had to admit that what Nan said was surely the truth. "What we'll have to do is find someone older to go with us," she sighed.

"I'm afraid that wouldn't be easy," Nan said. "Do you know of anybody?"

Nellie said no. Nan could not think of anyone either.

"Well," Nan said, "I was on my way down to Smilin' Syd's to get my bike fixed. It's in pretty bad shape. It won't steer right and the brake doesn't work very well, and there's a funny click in the wheel."

Nellie began to laugh. "It sounds like a broken-down wreck, all right," she said. "I'll go with you and see what Smilin' Syd has to say."

She went for her own bicycle, and the two girls rode downtown. Upon reaching the bicycle shop, they found Syd smiling broadly as usual. He was busy repairing a small tricycle.

"Well, hello, girls." His smile grew wider. "And what can I do for you today?" he asked.

Nan told Syd that several things seemed to be the matter with her bicycle. Would he please examine it carefully and tell her whether or not he could repair it? Syd took it into a rear room and was gone for about ten minutes. Finally he returned.

"I'm sorry, Nan," he said, "but I'm afraid nothing can be done about your bicycle. It's really not worth fixing. And as a matter of fact, it's not safe to ride. You might have an accident at any time. I'd be glad to give you a few dollars for it, though. I can use some of the parts to fix up other bikes."

Nan felt sad. Now, even if the Bobbsey twins could make the proposed bicycle trip, she would not be able to go along. Nellie sensed what her friend was thinking, and instantly she said:

· "Don't worry, Nan. You can use my bike."

"Oh, thank you, but I couldn't do that," Nan replied quickly. "If I do go, I want you to go too."

Smilin' Syd suggested that maybe Mr. Bobbsey would buy his daughter a new bicycle. On the chance that he might, Nan looked over all the bicycles which Syd had on display. But as she picked up one price tag after another, she was pretty sure that her father would say he did not want to spend so much money.

"Don't you have any used bikes?" Nan asked the shop owner.

"Not just now," Smilin' Syd replied regretfully. Then he brightened. "But I do know somebody who has one to sell. Why don't you run over to her house—it isn't very far from here, Nan. The name is Shelby—Jane Shelby."

"Oh, yes, I know her," said Nan. "Come on, Nellie, let's go see her right away!"

She thanked Smilin' Syd for the information, saying she would leave her own bicycle at his shop for the time being. She would let Syd know if she wanted him to buy it.

Nellie then asked the man if he would watch her bike until she came back. She would make the trip to the Shelby home on foot with Nan.

Bert, Freddie, and Flossie at that moment were trying out their own bicycles. Bert had gone off by himself, but the small twins had ridden together only three blocks from home. Presently Freddie said, "Flossie, watch me!"

He let go the handlebars and, spreading his arms wide, pedaled his bike along the sidewalk.

"Oh, be careful!" Flossie cried out the next minute. Freddie's front wheel had suddenly swerved, and he just missed bumping into a tree.

"Aw, nothing happened," Freddie boasted, but nevertheless took hold of the handlebars.

In a few minutes they turned onto a street which was on a sharp hill. Flossie was fearful about riding down it, but Freddie reminded her that if they did make the bicycle trip, there would be lots of hills to go up and down.

"We ought to practice," he told her. "Come on!"

He went ahead of Flossie, and for a time everything was all right. The small twins knew how to use their brakes. But suddenly Flossie began to go faster. When she tried to put on the brake, it didn't seem to work. She tried again, even standing up and pushing down hard on the pedals. But instead of stopping, she went faster than ever.

By now, Flossie was whizzing down the steep hill! Her brake just would not hold!

CHAPTER VII

NEW FRIENDS

AS FLOSSIE rushed down the hill on her bicycle, she screamed in fright. Her cries were heard by several people, who started racing toward her. But the little girl sped by before anyone could reach her. Finally a young woman who had been trimming a hedge near the bottom of the hill, called out:

"I'll get you!"

Running to the sidewalk, the young woman was just in time to meet Flossie, and forgetting any danger to herself, grabbed the little girl from the bicycle seat. The two swung around and fell to the grass.

Flossie had been saved from a bad accident!

"Oh-h-h!" was all Flossie could say, and then she began to sob.

"There, there, you're all right," the young woman said soothingly. She helped Flossie get up, looking closely at her, and asked, "Why, aren't you Flossie Bobbsey?"

The little girl stopped crying and said that

she was. Finally it occurred to Flossie to thank the young woman for saving her.

"I'm certainly glad I saw you coming," was the reply. "My name's Jane Shelby."

"Oh, Jane, you're wonderful!" Flossie cried, giving her new-found friend a big hug.

By this time Freddie Bobbsey had caught up to his twin. After learning she was all right, he went to get her bicycle. It had hit a tree and toppled over. And up the hill ran Nan Bobbsey and Nellie Parks. The girls had seen Flossie coming down, but since they had been some distance away, had not realized her bicycle was out of control.

Many people from the neighborhood had gathered around. Among them was Jane's brother, Allen Shelby.

Flossie explained that she had been trying out her bicycle. "Maybe we're going on a long trip," she said. "I wanted to be sure it was working all right."

Just then, Freddie returned with her bike. "Oh dear," Flossie wailed, seeing its twisted front wheel. "I'm afraid I can't go after all."

Allen Shelby examined the bicycle and said he was sure Smilin' Syd could replace the wheel in a jiffy. This made Flossie feel better and she went on with her story, telling about the missing Snowball and Charlie's bugle.

"We're going to try to find them," Flossie said. "That is, if our parents will let us."

Nan spoke up, saying that she was afraid not all the Bobbseys would be able to make the trip, because there was no older person to go with them. Suddenly Allen and Jane Shelby looked at each other. They nodded, and then Jane said:

"Maybe my brother and I can solve that problem, children."

The Bobbseys and Nellie looked at her questioningly. Then they asked what she meant.

Jane laughed and replied, "Allen and I are taking physical education courses at college. We can get extra points for supervising children in some kind of athletic project. So far, we haven't been able to find the right kind of project. But a bicycle trip with you would be perfect."

"You really mean it?" Freddie asked, his eyes very big. He turned to his sisters and Nellie. "Hurray! Now there's nothing to keep us from going on our bicycle trip!"

Nan said it all sounded wonderful to her, but a few things still had to be taken care of before they could start out. "For one thing, I have no bicycle." She told them how Smilin' Syd had said her old one was not safe for riding any more. With a smile, Nan then turned to

Jane Shelby. "I almost forgot. Smilin' Syd sent me to see a bicycle that you have for sale."

"He's right, I do have one," Jane replied. "I'll show it to you." The young woman laughed. "I've long since outgrown it. I have a bigger one now."

For the first time the Bobbseys noticed she was tall and very pretty, with shining dark hair. Her brother, too, was tall and a fine-looking young man.

All the children trooped to the Shelbys' garage where the bicycle for sale was kept. Nan was delighted with the trim-looking bike, which seemed to be in excellent condition.

"But," she sighed, "it may be more than my dad will want to pay."

"Maybe not," Jane replied with a smile. "I'm asking only fifteen dollars for it."

"Will you hold it for me until I ask Dad?" Nan asked eagerly.

"Certainly. And also tell your father and mother that Allen and I would like to talk to them about the trip any time they wish."

Freddie and Flossie were so excited they wanted to run home at once, so Nan offered to drop off Flossie's bicycle at Smilin' Syd's for repair.

Bert reached home soon after his sisters and brother, and was told the exciting news. The twins were glad when they heard the family car turn into the driveway. Dashing outside, they saw that Mr. Bobbsey had met his wife on the way home from his trip. The twins' mother had been out shopping.

Stopping the car, Mr. Bobbsey called out, "Now what's up? You children look excited!"

"Jane and Allen Shelby are going to get pointed for us at college!" Flossie yelled.

Everyone laughed, and Nan explained to her parents the part about the college points.

"Well, this is most interesting," said Mr. Bobbsey. "It begins to look as if your famous bicycle trip might take place after all. Mother was telling me what Bert and Charlie had in mind. But I didn't know that the rest of you wanted to go too."

Mrs. Bobbsey laughed. "I didn't know it either, Richard," she said. "These twins work fast!"

"We have to work fast," Freddie spoke up. "Because somebody else might find Snowball and the bugle."

"Well, Mary, what do you think?" Mr. Bobbsey asked.

Mrs. Bobbsey thought that Jane and Allen Shelby were fine young people. They were extremely good athletes and, she was sure, would be able to look after a group of children.

"Oh, Mother, you're scrumptious dumptious!" cried Flossie.

The twins' mother said that she would go to the telephone at once and talk over details with the Shelbys. There were a good many questions she would have to ask before giving her final consent.

Bert ran around to open the car door for his mother to alight, and walked with her to the kitchen door. Then he waited outside with the others. Flossie and Freddie were quiet as mice. They sat down on the grass, cupping their chins in their hands. It seemed to them as if their mother was never going to return, but about ten minutes later she came from the house. Mrs.

Bobbsey was smiling, which they were sure meant everything had been arranged.

"Good news!" she said. "You may go on the bicycle trip."

"Whoops!" shouted Freddie, immediately doing a double somersault on the lawn.

Flossie clapped her hands and danced around, while Bert began to whistle a merry tune. Nan was the only one who remained quiet.

"Is something the matter, dear?" her mother asked, noticing this.

At that moment Mr. Bobbsey came from the garage and joined his family. Turning to him, Nan repeated what Smilin' Syd had said about her old bicycle not being safe to ride any more.

"So I can't go, Daddy," Nan said. "Unless—unless I get another bicycle." Then she explained about the one Jane Shelby had for sale. "Could you possibly buy it for me?"

All the twins looked eagerly at their father, waiting for him to answer.

CHAPTER VIII

A STRANGE REQUEST

AS MR. BOBBSEY thought over his daughter's request, Nan held her breath. How she hoped her dad would let her buy the bicycle!

"Fifteen dollars, you say?" Then he smiled. "I'll tell you what, Nan. After supper we'll go over and take a look at Jane's bicycle. If it's worth that price, I'll buy it for you."

Nan was thrilled and as soon as supper was over, they started off for the Shelby home.

"Smilin' Syd said he would give me something for my old bike," Nan told her father. "I don't suppose it will be much, but it will help a little."

Mr. Bobbsey chuckled. "Every little bit helps."

When the twins' father saw Jane Shelby's bicycle, he said it certainly was a good bargain.

"Then—then you'll buy it?" Nan asked and, from her father's smiling face, knew the answer was yes.

After the sale had been concluded, Jane in-

vited Mr. Bobbsey and Nan into the house to
see her parents. When everyone was seated,
Mrs. Shelby remarked:

"This is quite a trip your family and mine
are undertaking."

"Yes, it is," Mr. Bobbsey agreed. "They don't
know how far they'll have to go, but it's almost
fifty miles from here to my brother Daniel's
farm."

Nan said they would go the whole distance
if necessary to find the missing cat and Charlie's bugle.

"I hope if anybody picked up Snowball, he's
being kind to our poor kitty," she said wist-
fully.

Her father turned to Jane and Allen. "I
know you'll take excellent care of all the children," he said. "They've promised to obey your
instructions, and I feel confident they'll live up
to their promise."

"I'm sure they will," said Jane, smiling, and
Allen nodded.

Just before lunch, the next day, Mrs. Bobbsey came back from shopping with a large
package. When it was opened the children
gasped in amazement. Their mother had purchased four pairs of very attractive leather
shorts for the bicycle trip. How soft and com-
fortable they looked!

"Oh, I just love mine," said Flossie. "Let's all put them on and show Dinah."

The twins did this and paraded into the kitchen. Sam was there also. He grinned broadly and said:

"My, you all sure look nice."

"Indeed you do," said his wife, beaming fondly, "and you'll be the best-dressed little bicycle riders in Lakeport."

Sam remarked that he had never seen any pants just like these.

"Oh, lots of children in Europe wear leather shorts when they ride bicycles," said Nan, who had read about this in a school book.

When the fashion parade was over, Freddie decided to get out his bicycle and try out the new pants for riding. He went up and down the block a couple of times and then concluded that this was a bit dull.

"I wish I had something to make a noise with," he thought. His mind traveled to Charlie's lost bugle. Suddenly the little boy said to himself, "I have an old toy bugle. I'll get that."

He hurried to his room and looked through his toy box. At the very bottom lay the bugle. He pulled it out and went back to the street.

Jumping onto his bicycle again, he rode off, blowing the toy bugle as loudly as he could.

Presently a young man who was hurrying

along stopped and hailed the little boy. He was very pleasant and asked if Freddie was playing a game.

"I'm just excited!" Freddie replied. "My sisters and brother and I are going on a long, long bicycle ride—fifty miles away!" he said.

"Hmmm." The young man looked interested. He then told Freddie he was a reporter for the *Lakeport News*. "This would make a good news story," he said. "Suppose you tell me more about it."

Freddie was very happy to do so. He mentioned the reasons for the trip, and the reporter, whose name was Mr. Price, began to write down some notes on a little pad. He asked where Freddie lived and said he would come to the house that afternoon with a photographer and take pictures of the twins. "And be sure to put on your new leather pants," he directed.

"Oh, I will," Freddie promised, "and I'll tell the others to wear theirs."

Waving good-by to Mr. Price, he pedaled home as fast as he could and burst into the house with his news. Everyone was excited on hearing it, but wondered a little if Freddie had the story straight. For this reason they did not notify the rest of the group.

Nevertheless, after lunch the children put on clean shirts and their new leather shorts and waited for the reporter to come. About two o'clock, Freddie, who was looking out the window, shouted, "Here he is!"

Climbing out of a car were Mr. Price and a photographer. They smiled.

Soon the children were posed in front of the house. Nan was standing beside her bike, Bert was just getting on his, and the small twins

were seated on theirs, with one foot on the ground to keep their balance.

"Ready!" the photographer said. "Smile!"

Click went the photographer's shutter. He took several shots to be sure of getting at least one good picture.

Next morning, the Bobbsey twins were awake early and went to the front porch to pick up the morning paper. There on the front page was their picture with an article about them!

BOBBSEY TWINS TO TAKE LONG BICYCLE TRIP

Freddie chuckled at his picture. "I look as if I were drinking sour lemonade!" he said.

"And I look," Flossie added, "as if I have the mumps!"

"Ours are good, Bert," said Nan.

The children went into the house, dressed, and came down to a breakfast of sausage and pancakes. They had just finished eating when the telephone rang. Dinah answered it and then called Nan.

"It's for you," she said.

"Hello," said Nan, expecting the caller would be one of her playmates.

But to her surprise she heard a woman's voice saying:

"This is Mrs. Elliott. You don't know me, but I've just read the article in this morning's paper about your family taking a bicycle trip. May I please come over to your house and talk about it? It's very important."

Nan replied that all the Bobbseys would be very glad to see Mrs. Elliott. While waiting for her to arrive, everyone wondered what she had to tell them. Would it be something to keep them from making the trip?

Almost an hour went by before Mrs. Elliott reached the Bobbsey home. With her was a very cute little girl whom she introduced as her daughter, Susan. She was four years old and at once Freddie and Flossie began to play with her. Meanwhile, Mrs. Elliott, seated in the living room with Mrs. Bobbsey, Bert, and Nan, addressed her remarks to them.

"When I read in the paper about your bicycle trip," the woman began, "I—I thought maybe you could help me out." A sad expression came into her eyes.

The three Bobbseys immediately decided to give the sweet-looking visitor any assistance they could. She was obviously very troubled about something. Now they listened intently as Mrs. Elliott continued:

"You see, I'm a widow. Susan is all I have. My husband and I had been putting money into a savings account in a bank over in Columbus. About two weeks ago I decided to buy a small house that's to be built on Beechcroft Hill."

As the visitor paused, Nan spoke up. "Why, we'll go past there on our trip."

"Yes, I know," Mrs. Elliott said.

The young widow went on to say that she had drawn all the money out of her savings account. There were six five-hundred-dollar bills. It was all to go toward buying the new home.

"Whew!" Bert whistled. "That's a lot of money!"

Mrs. Elliott said yes, it was. She tried hard to hold back the tears, but finally they began to roll down her cheeks.

"Please forgive me," she said. "I'm so dreadfully upset. You see, I lost the money! I don't know where exactly, but it must have been some place on the route that you'll be following on the bicycle trip."

Mrs. Elliott told them that some friends had driven her out to Beechcroft Hill to look over the property. Later they had gone on and stopped to have a picnic in a grove along the same road.

"It was not until I reached home that I discovered the money was gone," Mrs. Elliott said. "My friends and I have searched everywhere, but we didn't find even one of the bills."

The young woman paused, looked pleadingly at the Bobbseys, and said, "I just *must* get that money back. You will look for it, won't you?" she requested.

"We certainly will!" the Bobbsey twins chorused.

CHAPTER IX

THE WALKIE-TALKIE

WHILE Mrs. Elliott had been talking to Nan, Bert, and Mrs. Bobbsey, Freddie and Flossie had taken little Susan upstairs to show her their toys. The little visitor especially liked a rag doll which grinned in such a way that it always made people smile.

"May I play with this raggy doll while I'm here?" asked Susan, and Flossie said of course she might.

In Freddie's room they looked at a collection of stuffed toy animals. At once Susan saw a fuzzy white dog she wanted to put under her other arm. Freddie gave her permission.

"Now let's take her down to the kitchen to see Dinah," Flossie suggested to her twin. Turning to the little girl, she said, "Dinah makes wonderful cookies, Susan. You'll like them."

The twins led their small guest down the stairs and out to the kitchen. As they stopped at the door to the living room, Nan was just saying:

"Mrs. Elliott, we certainly will look for your lost money. We'll search everywhere for it."

Flossie and Freddie gathered from the living-room conversation that they would look for some lost money as well as Snowball and Charlie's bugle on their trip. How busy they would be!

Continuing to the kitchen, they found Dinah mixing something in a bowl. She smiled at the little visitor as Flossie and Freddie introduced her.

"We want to give Susan some cookies," said Flossie. "May we, please, Dinah?" she asked.

"Well, honey child, I'm making up a new batch," said the cook. "We're out of cookies, 'cept a couple."

She opened a cabinet door and took down a plate on which lay two cookies. One was in the shape of a doll, the other, a dog.

"Take these, honey," Dinah said kindly to Susan. "And the new batch will be baked soon."

Susan was happy with the two cookies Dinah had given her. She laid the rag doll and the stuffed dog down on a chair and took one cookie in each hand. She started to put the doll-shaped cookie to her lips, then changed her mind.

"They're too cute to eat," Susan said. "Dinah, I think I'll take both cookies home where I can look at them."

At this moment there was a whine at the screened back door and the children saw Waggo standing there. Dinah, who was near the door, opened it. The little fox terrier seemed very frisky and jumped around the kitchen. He looked up at Susan and gave a couple of barks as if to say, "How do you do."

Susan giggled and was just remarking, "What a nice dog!" when Waggo came up to her, and before she could move away, grabbed both cookies out of her hands. While she was still gasping, the dog swallowed them!

"You naughty, naughty dog!" Flossie scolded him. "And those were the last cookies, too!"

Susan burst into tears. Dinah tried to soothe her by saying she was going to bake the new batch of cookies at once. Then Susan might have all she wanted. But the little girl shook her head.

"We live far away from here, and Mommy and I have to go home pretty soon," she sobbed.

Poor Susan kept on crying. Flossie went up and put her arms around the little girl. "Please don't be unhappy," she said. "I'll tell you what —I'll give you this doll."

Flossie picked up the grinning rag doll from the chair and put it in Susan's arms.

"You mean I can have her for keeps?" she asked.

Flossie nodded, and Freddie, who had been standing by, wanted to help make Susan feel better too. Suddenly he picked up his toy dog and held it toward Susan.

"And take this too," he said.

Susan smiled through her tears. Happily she cried, "Oh, thank you!" and hugging the two toys tightly, ran into the living room to show them to her mother. Upon hearing about the gifts, Mrs. Elliott smiled.

"Susan, the Bobbseys are wonderful people," she said. "I just have a feeling they'll bring us good luck."

She arose from her chair and said that they must go home now. She wished the children luck on their trip and thanked the small twins for their gifts to Susan.

After they had gone, Mrs. Bobbsey suggested that the family have a little conference about what food the children should take on their trip.

"Are we going to eat canned food all the time?" asked Freddie, who had heard this was what campers usually do.

His mother smiled and said no. Mrs. Bobbsey felt that the bicycle riders should have one hearty meal a day and would ask the Shelbys to take the group to a restaurant for this meal.

"But I thought you would find it fun to have breakfast and either lunch or supper outdoors along the way," she said. "You mustn't build any fires, though, except under Jane's or Allen's direction."

All this time Bert had not been listening too closely. The boy had an idea which he was eager to talk over with his father. Telling his mother he was going down to the lumberyard, the boy said good-by.

Recently Bert had become interested in walkie-talkie sets. It had occurred to him that they might use one on the trip to keep in touch with their family. He had seen a set in the window of a store in Lakeport where surplus government supplies were sold. Now the boy walked past the store to see if the set was still there. It was!

Quickening his steps, Bert went on to his father's lumberyard, which always fascinated him. From time to time he had gone down there to help out. Now he could hear the sound of a large saw at work, so he took a route through the yard in order to reach Mr. Bobbsey's office.

What a busy place it was! Lumber was being

hoisted from a boat on the river and loaded onto two long trucks. Bert was very proud of his dad's business.

He found his father talking on the telephone and sat down to wait until he finished. Finally Mr. Bobbsey completed his conversation and said with a smile:

"What can I do for you, young man?"

Bert told his father the idea he had of using a short-wave set to send messages back and forth between the Bobbsey home and the bicycle travelers. He also mentioned the walkie-talkie set which could be bought for a low price.

"That sounds like an excellent plan, Bert," Mr. Bobbsey said. "I have a little spare time now. Suppose we go over to the store and look at the set."

He told his secretary where he was going, then he and Bert walked to the supply store. Mr. Bobbsey was very enthusiastic about the walkie-talkie set, and the clerk showed them how to operate it. When Mr. Bobbsey said they needed two sets, the man asked:

"Do you want them delivered or will you take them with you?"

Bert was eager to take the walkie-talkies along but could not carry both sets. Mr. Bobbsey offered to get the car and drive him home.

As they rode along, Bert said: "Dad, suppose we stop at Charlie's house and leave one set there. I'd like to try them out right away."

When Charlie saw Bert approaching with the walkie-talkie, he was very much excited. Charlie, as well as Bert, was mechanically minded. In a few minutes he knew exactly how to work the set.

"I'll go home now and we'll have a conversation back and forth," Bert told him.

He hurried off, and half an hour later was ready to begin the experiment. Bert had taken his walkie-talkie out to the back yard near a big tree. He turned it on and said:

"Calling Charlie Mason. Come in, Charlie. Over."

He flipped the instrument to the listening device and was thrilled to hear: "Charlie Mason answering Bert Bobbsey. Over."

The boys talked back and forth for some time. Presently Bert said:

"I sure hope we find your bugle, Charlie. You know, I still have a hunch Danny Rugg took that bugle."

The words were hardly out of his mouth when Bert heard a sudden movement behind him. The next instant something hit him on the back of the head.

Bert pitched forward and blacked out!

"I still have a hunch Danny Rugg took your bugle"

CHAPTER X

AN AMAZING BOMB

"BERT! Bert! What's the matter?" called Charlie Mason over the walkie-talkie set up in his back yard.

There was no response from Bert Bobbsey. At first Charlie thought the shortwave radio had gone dead. But the boy was sure he had heard Bert cry out and began to wonder if something were wrong.

"I'll phone the Bobbsey house," Charlie concluded, and rushed in to the telephone.

He made the connection and Nan answered. Quickly Charlie explained what had happened and suggested that Bert's twin go out to her back yard and see if her brother was all right.

"Let me know what you find out," he requested.

"I will," said Nan, hanging up.

She sped through the house and out to the back yard. Suddenly she stopped short. Bert lay on the ground unconscious. Calling at the top of her lungs for Mrs. Bobbsey, Nan rushed

71

to her brother's side. A shiver ran down her spine as she saw blood on the back of his head.

Mrs. Bobbsey, Dinah, and the small twins ran from the house. Mrs. Bobbsey knelt beside her son and examined him. Her face was very serious.

"We'll carry Bert into the house," she said.

As Freddie and Flossie looked on wide-eyed, Nan, her mother, and Dinah gently lifted Bert and carried him to the back door. Freddie held the door open. Bert was laid on the living-room couch.

"Nan, bring some ice water," her mother directed, "and, Dinah, find some gauze pads."

At this moment Bert stirred. He began to mumble and try to get up.

"You're all right, dear," said Mrs. Bobbsey, "but please lie still."

Bert mumbled again, opened his eyes, and looked at the group. Suddenly he put his hand to his head.

"It aches terribly," was all he said.

"I know, dear," said Mrs. Bobbsey, "but we'll do all we can to make it feel better."

When the cold water and gauze were brought, she washed the blood from the boy's head. Then she made a compress and laid it on the wound.

Presently Bert said he felt better. Although

his mother did not want him to talk, the boy insisted upon telling how someone had come from behind the tree and hit him.

"I don't know who it was," he said. Then, suddenly recalling the shortwave radio, he asked, "What happened to the walkie-talkie? Is it still there?"

In the excitement no one had thought of the set, and now Freddie dashed out to the yard. In a few minutes he came back to report that the instrument had been damaged!

Bert groaned and Mrs. Bobbsey put a stop to further conversation. Her son must rest for several hours. With Nan's aid, she and Dinah helped the boy up to his own bedroom and Mrs. Bobbsey said she would stay with him until the doctor came.

As soon as the other children reached the first floor, they began to talk excitedly but in hushed tones about what had happened. Nan suddenly remembered that she had promised to call Charlie, and went to the telephone. When Charlie heard the news, he said he would come right over and see if he could find any clues as to who Bert's assailant had been.

When he arrived, the four children went out to the yard. They could plainly see two sets of footprints around the big tree where Bert had been.

Charlie said, "If it was a man, I'd say he would have stolen the walkie-talkie, instead of almost smashing it. Do you know what I think?"

"Yes, I do," Freddie spoke up. "You think it was Danny Rugg."

Charlie admitted that this was exactly what was in his mind.

"This is why I think so," he said. "Just before Bert cried out, we were talking about my missing bugle. He was saying to me, 'I still have a hunch Danny Rugg took that bugle.'"

"Really?" Nan said. "Then I believe you're right, Charlie. Danny was probably hiding around here to find out what he could about our bicycle trip and was watching Bert with the walkie-talkie. When he heard my brother talk about his being suspected, it made him angry."

"And when Danny gets angry," said Charlie, "he gets rough. Maybe he didn't mean to hurt Bert so badly and break the walkie-talkie, but after he saw what he had done, he got scared and ran away."

Charlie was determined to find out and said he would go over to Danny's immediately. Upon reaching the Rugg house, he rang the bell over and over again. No one answered. He walked around the house, thinking someone might be in the back yard, but no one was in sight.

"I'll come back later," Charlie decided. But he had no better luck on his second trip that afternoon, and during the evening when he went over there, the house was in darkness.

Resolving not to give up, Charlie went to the Rugg home early the next morning. The family was not there, but a laundress was hanging out clothes. Charlie asked her where Danny was.

"He left early this morning on a bicycle trip," the woman replied.

Charlie's eyes popped! He immediately asked where the boy had gone.

"I think I heard him say something about Beechcroft Hill," the laundress answered.

Hearing this surprising news, Charlie ran all the way to the Bobbsey house. Bursting in, he told Nan, who was in the kitchen, what he had just learned.

"Oh dear!" said Nan. "So you think Danny has gone to look for your bugle?" Then she sighed. "I'd hate to have him find it. He might not give it back to you, Charlie."

"That's what I was thinking," said Charlie. "Would it be all right for me to see Bert?"

"I guess so," replied Nan. "He's sitting up in bed. The doctor says he'll have to stay there

most of today and we'll have to postpone our
bicycle trip."

"For how long?" Charlie asked.

"Oh, only one extra day," Nan replied.
"Bert wants to get up and start out right now,
but of course Mother won't let him. Besides,
the walkie-talkie's being fixed and won't be
ready till tomorrow."

When Bert heard Charlie's story, he was
more eager than ever to start the trip and find
out if Danny really had been his assailant.

"Whether he was or not, if Danny Rugg is
in the same woods we are," Charlie declared,
"there'll be trouble."

That evening Bert was allowed to get up for
supper, and had just joined the family when
Mr. Bobbsey came home. The twins' father
said he had some good news for them. He had
been in touch with the various property owners along the route the bicyclists would take.

"Every one of them has given permission
for you to camp on his particular property,"
he told them. "And you may do all the searching you like. Several of the farmers even offered to give you eggs and milk."

After supper, the front doorbell rang and
when Nan opened it, she saw an elderly man
standing there. He had twinkling blue eyes
and a very nice smile.

"Are you one of the girls who is going on the bicycle trip?" he asked.

"Yes, I am," Nan answered.

"Then may I come in and talk to you and your family about a proposition I have?" he requested.

Nan admitted the elderly gentleman and ushered him into the living room where her family was assembled.

"My name is Becker," he began. "I'm sorry to intrude, but I have something very important to talk to you about. I hope you won't mind."

Mr. Bobbsey had risen and asked their caller to take a seat. Mr. Becker explained that he was an inventor. Recently he had invented a new kind of fire-extinguisher bomb.

At this announcement, Freddie perked up at once. He crossed the room to seat himself on the floor directly in front of Mr. Becker.

"My extinguisher is instantaneous. When it's thrown into a fire, it will put out the blaze immediately."

"That sounds nifty," said Freddie admiringly.

Smiling at the small boy, Mr. Becker went on to say that a week before he had been making experiments in the country. A farmer who owned a large patch of woodland along the

route which the newspaper said the Bobbseys
were going to take on their bicycle trip had
asked him to put out a blaze.

"I had carried several of my bombs along,"
said Mr. Becker, "although only one was
needed to do the trick."

"Oh, I want to see you bomb a fire some-
time," Freddie interrupted.

"You certainly shall, young man," the inventor promised. "But now I must tell you the
purpose of my visit."

He then related that, upon returning home
the same evening, he was dismayed to find that
he was one bomb short.

"I must have dropped it in the woods," he
said. "I'm fearful that some campers may find
it. It's not marked and someone, not realizing
how powerful it is, might start a fire near by.
If the bomb should explode, he would get hurt.

"The farmer and I have searched everywhere, but we haven't found it. I had an ad
in the paper requesting that anyone who found
the bomb bring it back to me. But so far no one
has replied."

Mr. Becker paused and gazed at the Bobbsey
twins. "Would you hunt for my missing fire
extinguisher while you're on your bicycle
trip?"

Freddie jumped up excitedly from the floor.

"You bet!" he cried. "That's going to be my special job," he added enthusiastically. "I bet you didn't know I put out a fire in our garage all by myself with my pumper!"

The inventor chuckled, then he laid a hand on Freddie's shoulder. "Why, I think that's wonderful, little fellow. Tell you what," he said, "if you find my extinguisher, I'll make you a toy model. Then if you ever have another fire here, you can play fireman again and put it out."

After Mr. Becker had bid them good night, wishing the children luck in their search, Nan turned to her family.

"I wonder," she said thoughtfully, "who'll be the first lucky finder on our trip."

And Bert, Flossie, and Freddie wondered, too.

CHAPTER XI

"GO AWAY, SPIDER!"

FINALLY the big morning arrived! Today the Bobbsey twins and their friends would start on their bicycle trip. Bert had completely recovered and was eager to set off. At breakfast he remarked:

"I sure hope I find Charlie's bugle."

"And I'm going to get that fire extinguisher bomb," said Freddie.

Mrs. Bobbsey reminded her small son that the bomb was dangerous and that they must be extra careful.

Nan announced she was going to concentrate on trying to locate Mrs. Elliott's missing money.

"What bothers me is," Nan said, "that bills are green just like leaves and grass. If they were dropped in the woods, they'll be pretty hard to find."

From his pocket Bert took out a small magnifying glass. "Maybe this will help you, Sis." He grinned.

"Oh, I'm so glad you're taking that along," said his twin. "We may need it."

Mr. Bobbsey turned toward Flossie. "And how about my Fat Fairy?" he asked the little girl, calling her by his favorite nickname. "What are you going to hunt for?"

"Why, my blessed Snowball, of course," she replied.

The twins' mother smiled. "Well, I hope every one of you has success," she said.

After breakfast, Freddie trooped into the kitchen to check with Dinah on what was in his food basket. With a wide grin the cook nodded toward the basket.

"You-all just go 'head 'n' look, honey." She chuckled. "I promise you-all won't go hungry!"

The little boy peeped in at his supplies. There were cans of tomato and chicken soup, pineapple juice, jam, several jars of meat, and a loaf of bread.

"One thing's missing, Dinah," said Freddie. "I have to have a jar of peanut butter."

"That's right," said the cook. "How did I ever forget it? I'll put in some extra crackers, too."

Flossie came running out to check her basket also. She wanted to make sure that some of Dinah's homemade cookies were in it. "And please, Dinah," she said, "may I have some hard-boiled eggs?"

"I'll fix them for you, honey," Dinah agreed.

The children lined their bicycles up against the back porch. The food packages and extra clothes were put in wire baskets on the handle-bars. Next, the folding stove.

The sleeping bags, rolled into small bundles, were strapped on the twins' backs. When Flossie saw Freddie dressed in his short leather pants, his hiking boots, a little cap, and the pack on his back, she giggled.

"You look just like a flier with short pants and a parachute," she said.

Soon Bert and Nan came down the stairs in their riding clothes. Then Sam brought the walkie-talkie, which had been repaired. He said that if the twins had any trouble, they should call him over the shortwave set and he would come to help them.

As Nan thanked him, Flossie suddenly cried out, "Oh, I forgot Snowball's basket!"

The little girl ran to the garage. She was hardly inside the building, when the others heard her scream.

"What happened?" Mrs. Bobbsey gasped.

Everyone ran. Sam reached the garage first. Flossie was looking in the cat's basket on a shelf. Her eyes were wide with fright.

"Sam! Sam! Take it away!"

The kindly colored man looked inside the

The sleeping bags were
strapped on the twins' backs

basket. On the bottom of it was an enormous black spider. By this time the little girl was in tears.

Quickly Sam scooped up the spider on a shovel, and told the others that it was of a poisonous variety.

Hearing this, Flossie shrieked again and began to cry very loudly. "Did—he—did he ruin the basket?" she sobbed. "Will Snowball get poisoned if I put her in it?"

"Oh, no," said Sam with a chuckle. He disappeared behind the garage with the ugly spider.

As the group walked back toward their bicycles, Flossie seemed very serious. Freddie said to her, "Don't be sad. The spider didn't bite you."

But Flossie continued to look very sober and occasionally brushed away a tear. Bert decided to try cheering her up. After a few moments of thought, in which he was composing a ditty, he recited:

> "Little Miss Bobb-sey
> Got kind o' sob-sey
> While getting her basket for kitty;
> For there was a spider
> Right down beside her
> She didn't like it one bitty."

This made Flossie laugh and she wiped away

her tears. All the others laughed, too, and asked Bert to repeat his verse. Just as he finished, Jane and Allen Shelby rode toward them on their bicycles.

"Good morning!" they called to the Bobbseys and got off their bikes.

"We're all ready," Nan reported. "Nellie and Charlie should be here soon."

Nellie Parks arrived in a few minutes. Around her neck was a strap to which was attached a camera. She jumped from her bicycle and said good morning. Then, holding out the camera, she said:

"This is my father's new camera. He's lending it to us for the trip. And guess what! When you take pictures with it, they're developed right away. Want to see how it works?"

"Oh, yes!" the others chorused.

Nellie had the Bobbsey twins and the Shelbys line up near the porch and then snapped a picture. She went to the shaded side of the house and in a few minutes returned with a snapshot. Everyone crowded around to, see the result.

"Oh, how wonderful!" Nan exclaimed. "Maybe we can use the camera to get some clues."

"That's a swell idea," said Bert.

The group chatted a few minutes more, then

Allen Shelby asked where Charlie was. Bert said he had not heard from his friend, though he had expected him long before this.

"I'll go telephone his house to see what's happened," Bert offered.

He hurried inside and put in the call. Mrs. Mason answered. When she heard that Charlie had not arrived at the Bobbsey home, she became alarmed.

"Why, my son left here an hour ago," she said. "He was going directly to your house!"

CHAPTER XII

MONKEYS AND ELEPHANTS

BERT BOBBSEY'S heart began to thump with worry. Had something happened to Charlie Mason just as they were ready to leave on the trip?

"I'll look for Charlie," he told Mrs. Mason.

Rushing outside, Bert told the others what he had just learned. Jumping onto his bicycle, he started off, saying he would find his friend. Nan, too, jumped on her bicycle. Down the street they went, around the corner and to the next street, which led to the Mason house. Charlie was nowhere in sight.

When they reached his home, Mrs. Mason was standing on the front walk. She said she had searched the house, grounds, and garage thoroughly, but her son was not to be found.

Bert had an idea. "Maybe he went over to Ruggs' to see if Danny is back."

The two cyclists hurried off toward Danny's house. Charlie's bike was not there, and when they rang the bell, there was no answer.

"Now where shall we look?" Bert asked.

Nan said that perhaps something had gone wrong with Charlie's bicycle and he had gone to Smilin' Syd's to have it fixed. She and her twin jumped onto their bicycles once more and headed for the repair shop.

Nan had guessed right! Inside was Charlie, fully dressed for the trip. Smilin' Syd was tinkering with the rear wheel of the boy's bicycle.

"Charlie!" Bert cried, running inside. "You sure gave us all a scare. We thought something had happened to you."

Charlie said he was very sorry. He glanced up at the clock and remarked that he had not realized so much time had elapsed.

"Just as I started off," he explained, "the rear wheel of my bike began to wobble. I didn't think I'd better take the trip until it was fixed."

Bert asked Smilin' Syd how much longer the job would take.

"Not more than five minutes," the repair man replied, grinning broadly.

Five minutes later, the three cyclists, waving good-by, left the shop. They rode quickly to the Bobbseys' home, and Charlie immediately telephoned his own house to assure his mother he was safe and sound.

"All aboard!" Freddie shouted, climbing onto his little bicycle.

The group then lined up. Allen Shelby was to lead the way, with Freddie directly behind him, Flossie coming next, then Nan, then Nellie. Behind her was Bert, then Charlie. Jane Shelby would bring up the rear.

Flossie, seeing the arrangement, called out, "I always thought it was ladies first."

Jane Shelby laughed. She said that every first-class expedition always had a brave man in front to pave the way. Flossie felt better and settled on the seat of her bicycle.

"Good-by! Good-by!" the grownups and the children shouted to one another.

Mrs. Bobbsey ran over to give each of the twins an extra kiss. Then they set off.

"Good luck! Good luck to all of you!" Dinah and Sam called.

By this time several neighbors and playmates had come from their homes and now stood along the sidewalks.

As the bicyclists passed them, they waved.

Soon the streets of Lakeport were left behind and the cyclists found themselves on a country road. Allen had a map which Mr. Bobbsey had given him, and about half an hour later he turned into a very narrow road.

As they rode along, Jane Shelby noticed how

well all the children handled their bicycles. She marveled particularly at Freddie and Flossie and decided they were the best young bicyclists she had ever seen.

The riders had gone about a mile, when suddenly they heard the scream of a siren. They looked up the road and saw a motorcycle policeman approaching at high speed.

In a couple of minutes the policeman roared up to them and stopped. He waved the cyclists to the side of the road, and told them to pull their bikes up onto the wooded embankment. Everyone obeyed, then waited breathlessly to hear what he was going to say.

To their relief, he smiled. "I hope I didn't frighten you," he said. "But I have orders to clear the road for a little while. Some animals are being transferred to the Lakeport Zoo and they're coming this way."

"Oh, how scrumptious!" exclaimed Flossie.

Within five minutes the children could see a line of big trucks coming. Soon the first one passed them. In it were two white polar bears.

"The poor things!" said Flossie. "They look hot. I guess they'll be glad to get to the Lakeport Zoo where they can sit on a cake of ice."

As everyone laughed, the next truck rumbled by.

"Lions!" shouted Freddie. "And do they look mad!"

The two lions in the cage were pacing back and forth, looking longingly toward the woods.

"Oh, here come the elephants!" Nan called.

As the huge animals lumbered past the children they noticed that the second elephant was holding the tail of the one in front of him with his trunk. The one behind, in turn, had hold of his tail and so it went all down the line.

There were six elephants altogether, the leader being a large old fellow and at the end of the line a cute baby elephant.

"Oh, isn't she darling!" Nellie exclaimed, and at once focused her camera for a picture.

At the sound of the girl's voice, the little elephant turned its head and blinked at her. Quickly Nellie snapped the picture.

Bert and Charlie were grinning. Their eyes were turned toward the last truck in the procession. This carried a very large cage of monkeys. The lively little animals, chattering and squealing, were climbing around the bars of the cage.

"Oh, I wish they wouldn't go by so fast," said Bert. "I love to watch monkeys."

As if in answer to his wish, there was a shout from somewhere near the head of the parade, and one by one the trucks stopped. A man who had been walking beside the elephants came over to the bicyclists.

"Sorry to hold you up," he said, "but we have to rest the elephants awhile."

"Oh, we're glad!" Flossie told him. "Now we can play with the elephants and the monkeys longer."

Allen asked the man if this would be all right, and he said, "Sure, go ahead. They're all trained except that big monkey sitting by himself in a corner of the cage. Bringo's a kind of ferocious old fellow when it comes to being near people. Stay away from him."

The children looked at the elephants first. But since one could not really play with them, they all moved on to see the monkeys, except Freddie.

The little boy had suddenly gotten an idea. Knowing that elephants love to eat peanuts, he decided to share some of his peanut butter with them. Going to his basket, he unpacked the jar. He struggled with the lid for several minutes, then, unable to get it off, walked up to Allen Shelby.

"Would you please take this off?" he requested.

The young man did not question Freddie's request. He merely assumed the little fellow was hungry and was going to make himself a sandwich.

As soon as the jar was opened, Freddie ran back to where the elephants were. He found a stick shaped like a little paddle and stuck it down into the peanut butter. Scooping up a good quantity of it, he held the stick toward the baby elephant.

Swoosh!

The peanut butter was swept up by the little trunk and transferred to the baby's mouth. Instantly the animal held its trunk toward Freddie for a second helping of peanut butter.

"Just one more bite," said Freddie with a

grin. "I want to save some for the others."

But the small elephant seemed to enjoy the peanut butter so much that Freddie kept on feeding him. All of a sudden he noticed that the jar was completely empty! He shrugged, telling himself it had been more fun giving it to the baby elephant.

He had just started to walk toward the monkeys' cage when he heard his sister Nan give a loud scream.

Bringo, the ferocious monkey, had reached through the cage with both arms and was holding Nan tightly by the hair!

CHAPTER XIII

A MISCHIEVOUS ANIMAL

CRYING in pain, Nan Bobbsey tried to pull away from the vicious monkey. But he held on tightly to her hair.

"Stop it! Let her go!" screamed Flossie, who was standing next to her sister.

The Shelbys had been on the other side of the cage, but dashed around the corner. Allen cuffed the monkey's wrists. Bringo squealed, but still would not let go of Nan's hair. Reaching inside the cage, the young man gave him a hard slap on the back. This made the monkey release his hold.

Nan staggered to the embankment and sat down, holding her hands to her head. Jane Shelby massaged Nan's sore scalp to stimulate the circulation. All this time the enraged monkey screamed and chattered at them.

"Oh, you're awful bad!" Flossie scolded him, but kept a safe distance away, so that Bringo could not touch her.

By now the monkey's keeper, who had

walked ahead a distance to speak to the elephant trainer, had rushed back. He made sure that Nan was all right and then went to calm the monkey.

"Tush! Tush!" he said sternly. "Bringo, aren't you ashamed of yourself?"

But Bringo did not seem to be the least bit ashamed. He jumped around the cage, annoying all the other monkeys.

"I guess I'll have to go in there and quiet that old fellow," the keeper said finally.

He unlocked the cage door, opened it a little way, and squeezed himself inside. Everyone was so busy watching him, wondering what Bringo might do next, that it was only Flossie who noticed that one of the small monkeys had crawled between the man's feet and through the cage door. Before she could cry out, the little animal had escaped from the cage.

He leaped to the embankment, paused for a second to look around, then ran quickly into the woods. Flossie rushed after him.

"Come back! Come back!" she cried.

But the monkey paid no attention. He scampered up a tree, sat on a limb, and looked down at her.

"Oh, you mustn't run away!" Flossie told him.

Everything had happened so fast that it was

not until now that the others realized the monkey was loose. The Bobbseys and their friends crowded around the tree, staring up at him.

"I'll get him down," Bert offered.

The boy shinned up the tree and along the limb on which the monkey was sitting. But just as Bert made a grab for him, the mischievous animal jumped to the next tree.

"My turn." Charlie chuckled. "I'll bring that little fellow down!"

But this was easier said than done. Charlie had the same experience as Bert. It certainly looked as if the monkey had gained his freedom for good.

The keeper, having finally calmed Bringo, now came to help make the capture. He talked soothingly to the monkey, whose name was Dodo, and even jabbered at him in an odd language which the children could not understand. They concluded it must be monkey talk! But still the little creature up among the branches refused to come down.

"Let me try something," said Nellie.

She dashed back to her bicycle and took a banana from her food package. Hurrying back to the tree, she quickly peeled the banana. Then she held it up as high as she could toward the monkey.

Seeing this luscious tidbit which he loved

so much, Dodo could not hold out any longer. He swung from branch to branch until he was only a few feet above Nellie, then leaped to her shoulder and began to nibble the banana.

As the others watched in delight, the keeper walked closer and closer, ready to grab the monkey as soon as he had finished eating. As he took the last bite, the man said:

"Come now, Dodo, you must go back into your cage."

But as he reached out his hands for him, Dodo bared his teeth, then settled down around Nellie's neck. The man laughed.

"You've certainly captured Dodo's affections, little girl," he said.

The keeper tried a second time to coax the monkey to come, but he still refused, clinging tightly to Nellie. The girl looked pleadingly at the man and asked:

"Do you think I could keep her?"

The other children were surprised at the request, but what fun it would be to have a monkey along on their bicycle trip!

"Oh, I'm afraid that wouldn't work out very well," Jane Shelby spoke up quickly.

Nellie looked disappointed until the monkey's keeper said, "You children may all see Dodo in the Lakeport Zoo."

Sighing, Nellie lifted the monkey from her

"Do you think I could keep her?" Nellie asked

neck and handed him to the man. He put Dodo back in the cage, and a few moments later an order was given for the animal procession to move on. Soon the parade was on its way down the road. The children watched it, determined to visit the zoo and see their new animal friends as soon as they returned to Lakeport.

They took their bicycles from the embankment and mounted them once more. They pedaled quickly along the narrow country road. There had not been a house in sight for some time, but up ahead they saw one with a sign in front. At this moment, Freddie announced that he was starving.

"Shall we stop now and eat?" Allen called back to his sister.

Jane said that perhaps the farmhouse up ahead with the sign was a restaurant. She thought that if it were, they could have their big meal in the middle of the day and prepare their own supper when they camped for the night.

"Good idea," Allen agreed.

As they drew closer to the farmhouse, it proved to be a restaurant indeed. The sign said:

DELICIOUS COUNTRY DINNERS

Everyone was famished. They pulled up in

front of the farmhouse and Allen went inside to inquire about a meal. He came out presently to announce that by the time they all had washed, and combed their hair, dinner would be ready.

My, how good everything tasted! The farmer's wife, who did the cooking, said that everything on the menu was fresh from the farm. "My husband raises the animals, the vegetables, and the fruit," she told the travelers. "I cook them and my daughter serves them."

Freddie thought this over a moment, then he asked, "And do you make a lot of money?"

The woman, plump and jolly, laughed, saying that money was not everything in life. To have happiness was far better.

"We serve the best meals we possibly can and we charge a reasonable price," she said. "We make a fair profit and live comfortably. What more could anyone want in this life?"

The Bobbseys and their friends agreed with this wholeheartedly. When they finished eating, they thanked the farmer's wife and said good-by. Then they pedaled straight along the dusty country road. At four o'clock, Jane called ahead to her brother that she thought they should stop.

"We've really come a long distance," she said, "much farther than I thought we would make in one day. Suppose we find a place to camp, and after we rest awhile, let's play some games."

Allen selected a nice spot along a brook. There were lovely big shade trees all around and the campers wheeled their bicycles a little distance in from the road. The place was apparently part of a large farm, for in the distance they could see a house and a barn.

After consulting the map, Allen told the others that they were now on the Mosswood estate.

Bert consulted his wrist watch every once in a while. He had told his father that at six o'clock sharp he would use the walkie-talkie and tell Mr. Bobbsey where they were. In a few minutes he excused himself from the game and rigged up his shortwave set. Soon he and Mr. Bobbsey were talking to each other.

Bert told him what an interesting day they had had, and Mr. Bobbsey laughed heartily when he heard about the animals' parade. He said everyone at home was fine and then added, "Where are you?"

Bert replied that they were camping on the edge of the Mosswood estate.

"The Mosswood estate?" his father repeated. "I'm very sorry to hear that, Bert. You must all move away from there at once!"

CHAPTER XIV

A GRUFF CARETAKER

WHEN Mr. Bobbsey said that the campers would have to leave the Mosswood estate, Bert quickly asked over the walkie-talkie, "Why, Dad?"

His father said that Mosswood Farm was dangerous. Only an hour before, Sam had mentioned to a friend of his that the children were on a bicycle trip. Hearing what their route was, Sam's friend had told him there was a vicious dog at Mosswood. Bert gulped.

"I understand the dog is chained up most of the time," Mr. Bobbsey told him. "But he's strong enough to tear loose. He's part wolf and everyone for miles around is afraid of him."

Bert asked his father why the owner of Mosswood had given permission for the group to stay there, if he knew it would not be safe. Was Sam really sure this was the Mosswood estate his friend had meant?

"Yes," Mr. Bobbsey replied. "Probably the owner is sure his dog can't get loose. But Sam's friend goes out there to make deliveries. He says this dog is really mean. I'd feel better if you'd move on a few miles."

"All right, Dad. We will," Bert promised.

When Jane and Allen Shelby heard Mr. Bobbsey's message they ordered everyone to pack up. Just as they were ready to leave, they heard barking in the distance. Quickly they hopped onto the bicycles and set off down the road.

Freddie could not resist the temptation to turn around and see if the animal were behind them. As he looked back over his shoulder, his eyes grew wide with fright. A large dog was leaping down the road toward them!

Between his fright and not looking where he was going, Freddie's handlebars suddenly twisted out of his grasp. At the same moment the bike hit a little rut in the road.

The next instant Freddie somersaulted over the bars!

"Oh, Freddie!" Flossie screamed.

Everyone stopped, and Nan ran forward to

help her little brother. He had landed in soft dirt and did not seem to be hurt. But he looked a bit dazed.

"Are you all right?" his sister asked.

"I—I guess so," said Freddie.

The others had gathered around, but Allen had never taken his eyes off the monstrous dog which was now much closer to them.

"Come on, everybody! Quick!" the young man yelled. "Jane, get the girls started."

The girls mounted their bikes and pedaled off like lightning. The boys followed closely. At this moment they heard someone whistling.

"Don't turn around!" Jane commanded, as she saw the children in front of her start to turn their heads. "Keep going!"

But she herself did risk a look back and, to her relief, noticed a man with a whip dash from the fields and yell at the dog. The next instant he had hooked a leash onto the animal's collar and was holding him tightly.

"Thank goodness!" the young woman exclaimed and called to those ahead that they were safe now.

Everybody stopped and pulled up to the side of the road to catch their breath. After they had rested a few minutes and had overcome their fright, Jane asked her brother:

"How far is it from here to Beechcroft Hill?"

Allen consulted his map and said it was only three miles.

"Then I think if you children feel able to ride that far, we'd better go there," Jane said.

Nan looked at her small brother and sister. Both of them looked very weary and Freddie was dirt-covered and mussed up. "How do your legs feel? Tired?" she asked them.

The small twins replied that they were all right, and Freddie added manfully, "If you big folks can take it, so can I!"

As they pedaled toward Beechcroft Hill, the sun began to set. It was a large ball of fire surrounded by beautiful salmon- and aqua-colored clouds.

"The sky looks like fairyland," Flossie remarked, and the others agreed with her.

When they arrived at Beechcroft Hill, Jane and Allen hunted for a good camp site. Finally they found one a couple of hundred feet in from the road. It was in a little pine grove and the thick carpet of needles on the ground made it an ideal sleeping spot.

Freddie declared he was hungry, so they all had sandwiches, tomato juice, and fruit. Then sleeping bags were rolled out. The small twins were just about to crawl into theirs when Nan noticed a flashlight beam bobbing through the dark woods. "I guess we're going to have company," she said.

Everyone waited to see who was approaching. Suddenly it occurred to Jane that the person might not be friendly and she whispered

this to her brother. He ordered all the flash-
lights put out in the hope the intruder would
not notice them.

Everyone sat motionless watching the flashlight beam still coming toward them.

The person holding the light seemed to be
very familiar with the woods. Soon they knew
that they could not escape being discovered.
The light was almost on them. Then a few moments later they heard an exclamation:

"I thought so! More trespassers!"

Bert and Nan gasped in amazement. They
recognized the voice as that of Jed Rustum, the
gruff caretaker whom they had met when they
first came to Beechcroft Hill.

Now he shined his flashlight full in their
faces.

"So you're here again!" he shouted. "I told
you to stay off this property!"

"I know you did," Bert spoke up, "but—"

"There are no buts about it," Jed Rustum
screamed in a high shrill voice. "Get out of
here—all of you!"

"But we have permission to camp here," Bert
went on quickly.

"You do, eh?" the caretaker said, a look of
surprise coming over his face. "I don't believe
it. Show me some proof!"

Bert Bobbsey's face fell. He had no proof!

CHAPTER XV

THE SEARCH STARTS

JED RUSTUM cackled triumphantly. "See, I told you," he gloated. "You got no right on Beechcroft Hill. Now pack up and get out as fast as you can!"

"But we're doing no harm," said Jane Shelby. "We're only staying for one night—"

"Just a minute," her brother broke in. He had been searching through his pockets. Now he pulled out a letter and said with a smile, "I think this will fix everything up."

The others gazed at him, astounded. He explained that just before leaving, Mr. Bobbsey had given him several letters. These were from people along the route the bicyclists were planning to take, granting permission to stay on their property. Allen said this was one from the owner of Beechcroft Hill. He extended it to Jed Rustum to read.

"Why—why—" said the caretaker, looking more crestfallen each moment as he read on. "Why—why— This looks real."

"Of course it's real," said Allen. "Now may we stay?"

The elderly man shook his head and mumbled to himself, "Why couldn't he tell me what's goin' on?" Then he said aloud to the others, "Well, since you got permission, I guess I got to let you stay. But don't make your visit too long."

Nan walked up to the old man. She reminded him of the bugle which they were trying to find and asked if he had seen any sign of it.

"No, I ain't," Jed Rustum replied irritably. "Is that why you're here again—after that pesky bugle?"

Nan said yes and that they were going to make a thorough search of the woods the following morning.

"Well, I don't think you'll find it," the man replied. "These here woods have been so full of people lately, that if there was any bugle around, I'm sure somebody's picked it up by now."

Charlie gulped. He hoped Jed Rustum was wrong!

"Go ahead and hunt anyhow," the man said with a shrug. "But take care in these woods. We don't want any fires or any accidents."

The group promised to be careful. Then,

without another word, Jed Rustum turned on his heel and walked off. For a few minutes the campers could see his light weaving in and out among the trees. Then it was gone.

Suddenly Bert burst into laughter. "Allen, it was sure lucky that Dad gave you that letter. We might have been riding all night!"

"And I can use a lot of sleep," said Charlie, yawning. "I want to get up early and start looking for my bugle."

Everyone slept soundly for the rest of the night and was awakened in the morning by the chirping of birds. As Flossie opened her eyes, she was reminded of the time she had been lost and spent the night alone in the woods. But the little girl had not been frightened, because of the friendly birds.

"I'm going to give these birds some of my breakfast," Flossie told herself, crawling out of her sleeping bag and rubbing her shorts to smooth out some of the wrinkles.

To her surprise and that of the other children, Allen Shelby was not around. Jane explained that he had gone off to a near-by farmhouse for fresh eggs and milk. She already had the little stove going and was frying bacon.

"Ummm, it smells good!" said Freddie.

In a few minutes Allen returned, carrying three quarts of milk and two dozen eggs. Soon everyone was seated in a circle, enjoying the tasty food.

Flossie had already collected several birds around her by feeding them tidbits of toast. It was such a pretty scene that Nellie decided to take a picture of it. She snapped one and when she showed the finished picture, everyone was delighted. In the bill of one bird was a long piece of fried egg-white which Flossie had slipped to it.

After all the scraps had been cleaned up, and the extra food packed away, Jane suggested that before starting their search, they hide their bicycles and their equipment.

"That's a good idea, Sis," Allen agreed.

He and the boys hunted around for a likely spot. After a little while they found a small, rocky cave. It was an ideal place in which to put their things. Tucking them out of sight, the boys got branches and covered up the cave opening, so that it would not be noticed.

They returned to the others, who were ready to start the search in the woods.

"I think it would be a good idea if we spread out and walked about four feet apart left and right," said Allen. "In this way, we shouldn't miss anything."

The campers lined up in the same order as they had taken while riding their bicycles.

"Ready! Set! Go!" Freddie shouted.

Eagerly the group began their hunt. Although each one was intent upon finding a particular thing, all of them kept their eyes open for any of the missing articles. Every bush was examined. And every big tree was walked around. The searchers scratched among the leaves on the ground and looked up among the branches.

It was difficult to keep in a straight line, and presently Freddie found himself a little distance ahead of the others. Suddenly he almost stepped into the remains of a fire. In the center of it lay a small glass ball, black with soot.

"Hey, everybody, come quick!" Fireman Freddie shouted. "I think I've found the extinguisher!"

The others rushed forward and gazed at the ashes. As the little boy pointed out his find, the others agreed that perhaps he really had found what was left of Mr. Becker's lost property.

Allen bent down and felt the ashes. They were cold, so the fire was not a recent one.

Freddie was already leaning down and picking up the glass ball, which he discovered had a jagged opening on one side. He turned it over and said there was some small printing on it.

"I can't read it," he told Bert. "Look at it through your magnifying glass."

His brother took the glass from his pocket and held it near the glass ball. A moment later he burst out laughing.

"It says," Bert explained, " 'Ritelite Lamp Company.' It's a broken light bulb."

The others laughed too—that is, everyone except Freddie. He was completely crestfallen.

"But I'll find Mr. Becker's extinguisher yet," he determined, and began to march on.

The searchers walked for some time without seeing anything else that might be a clue to the missing articles. Every once in a while Flossie would call out Snowball's name hopefully, but there was never an answering meow.

Soon they came to a small stream and Jane said they could ford it easily by skipping across the stones which appeared above the water. The twins and their friends thought this was great fun as they started out over the brook.

Bert and Charlie, feeling a little silly, began to dance a jig, making the younger children laugh. Freddie started to imitate them, but when he almost lost his balance, the little boy gave up the stunt.

Flossie, however, did a few dance steps she had learned in school. Pretending to be a ballet dancer, she gave a flying leap from one stone to another. But the little girl did not quite make it.

Plop! She landed sitting in the water!

Quickly Nan pulled her small sister out of the shallow stream and found she was not very wet. Her leather shorts and heavy shoes had saved her from a thorough soaking! And before long she was practically dry.

On and on went the searchers. They were having no luck at all but were enjoying themselves very much nevertheless. As they reached the crest of a little rise of ground in a woodsy section, Charlie suddenly grabbed Bert's arm.

"Look over there!" he said excitedly. "In those bushes. I saw two faces. And I'm sure they were Danny Rugg's and Jack Westley's!"

CHAPTER XVI

AN UNPLEASANT SURPRISE

"YES, I'm sure it was Danny and Jack hiding in those bushes," said Charlie.

"Golly," Bert said. "If it was, now's my chance to find out whether Danny knocked me out and nearly smashed my walkie-talkie!"

"Come on!" Charlie urged.

The boys asked Allen's permission. He said he would go with them and the three dashed off through the woods. Way ahead, the pursuers could see the two figures. But a moment later they disappeared from sight.

"We mustn't lose them!" Bert cried, running faster.

Although he and his companions could see no one, they could hear thrashing noises in the underbrush ahead, and followed the sound.

"There they are!" Charlie yelled.

There was no question about it. Now the two boys ahead could be seen plainly. They were indeed Danny and Jack!

But the bullies had a good head start, and

besides, they seemed to be more familiar with the woods than Bert and Charlie. In a couple of minutes Danny and Jack were out of sight again, and though the others ran as quickly as they could, they could not catch up. Soon there was only silence up ahead. Bert and his friends had to admit that the other boys had got the better of them.

"Well, I'll get him yet!" Bert determined.

Allen said that he thought they should return to their camp site as it was nearly lunch time.

The girls and Freddie were on their way to the spot where they had left their bicycles and the food. But at the moment they were much farther from it than the three boys.

It seemed like a long walk back to their camp site. While they were still some distance from it, suddenly all of them jumped. Almost directly in front of them they had heard a loud *moo*.

"Oh, I hope it's a friendly cow," Nan said.

Jane changed their course a little, but in a few minutes the same *moo* sounded in front of them again. This time she and Nan and Nellie exchanged glances. This was very strange!

The next minute she laughed merrily and so did Nan and Nellie. Flossie and Freddie looked at them in surprise.

"What's so funny?" Freddie asked.

For answer, Nan pointed ahead. Standing near a tree were three figures. One of them had just raised his head, pursed his lips, and in a moment cried loudly, *"Moo!"*

"Bert Bobbsey!" Flossie cried out. "You're just playing jokes on us!"

"A very good joke, I'd say," Jane remarked. "We all were fooled for a while."

The whole group went on together, with Bert telling Jane and the others about seeing Danny and Jack.

"So they are in these woods!" Nan said, worried.

In a few minutes they reached their camp site. Jane and the older girls went into the cave to get some food. In a couple of minutes the others heard them cry out.

"I wonder what's up," Bert said as he and the rest rushed over, reaching the cave just in time to meet the girls coming out.

"The food! Most of it's gone!" Nan cried despairingly.

"Gone!" the boys chorused. Then Bert added quickly, "Are the bikes still there?"

"Yes, they are."

The campers had several guesses as to who might have taken the food. Bert and Charlie were sure that it was Danny and Jack. But Nan did not agree. She said that if they had wanted to play a trick, the mean boys probably would have taken the bicycles too.

"I believe you're right," said Jane. "It's my guess that one or more wild animals helped themselves to the food."

Allen shook his head. "Animals wouldn't carry off packages of food. They'd tear them open on the spot and eat the contents."

The others knew this was true. Then who could the thief have been?

"I think," said Allen, "it may have been Jed Rustum. He doesn't want us around here. What better way to discourage us than to take our food?"

"That sounds reasonable," his sister admitted. "But what are we going to do for lunch?"

"Why don't I ride over to the farmhouse and get us something to eat?" Allen suggested.

Jane said this was a good plan, and Allen mounted his bike. While they were waiting for Allen to return, the others discussed what had happened. Jane felt that at no time should all of them go off again and leave their supplies unguarded. It was bad enough to have their food taken, but suppose somebody *had* helped himself to all the bicycles!

"We'd sure be out of luck," said Bert.

Although Jane did not say so aloud, she

thought that the small twins seemed pretty tired. She suggested that the girls and Freddie stay with her and let Allen and the older boys continue the search alone in the afternoon. They all agreed to this.

In a short time Allen returned, his bicycle basket piled high. In it were ham sandwiches, a large jar of apple sauce, a chocolate cake, milk and supper supplies.

After the delicious lunch Allen, Bert, and Charlie set off. For a while they walked along together, then Allen thought he saw something move to his left and went off to investigate.

Bert and Charlie, however, did not notice where he was going and stalked ahead. Then they heard a noise behind them and turned, expecting to see Allen. But the young man was not in sight.

"What was that?" Charlie asked.

Bert had not had time to reply when the same sound came from their right. Again they looked through bushes and among the trees but could see nothing.

"It's probably an animal," Bert concluded.

Just then the sound came again. This time from almost directly in front of Bert and Charlie. By now they had reached the top of a small hill in the woods and stopped to look down the other side.

Suddenly Bert's eyes popped and he grabbed Charlie's arm. "Over there!" he hissed, pointing to a hollow tree ahead of them.

Together the two boys cried out: "The bugle!"

Bert and Charlie started down the hill toward the old tree. The next second the boys could hardly believe what they saw.

An arm, reaching around from behind the tree, snatched away the bugle!

CHAPTER XVII

A PUZZLING SITUATION

THE snatching of Charlie's bugle from the hollow tree was so unexpected that Bert and his friend still could not believe their eyes. The arm and the bugle had disappeared instantly, and there was not a sound.

Both boys dashed forward, sure of catching up with the thief. But when they looked behind the tree, there was no sign of him.

Since the ground was stony, there were no footprints. The boys peered up into the trees, but saw no one. And the clumps of bushes near by were not big enough for concealment—anyone running off could have been seen.

"It's just plain crazy!" Bert remarked. "You'd think the thief had gone up in smoke!"

"It's almost spooky," Charlie said. "It seemed like—like the arm that took the bugle didn't have any body and just floated away!"

At this moment Bert thought he saw a slight movement on the ground not very far from where they were standing. He looked hard at the spot. Yes, he was not wrong. A large stone was actually moving! Nudging Charlie, he pointed and whispered, "I think I've found the hiding place."

The two boys watched intently. The stone was motionless now, but there was no doubt that it had heaved up a bit, then fallen back into place.

Charlie, incredulous, said into Bert's ear, "Do you think the thief's hiding under the stone?"

Bert said yes, there was probably a pit underneath the rock. Anyhow, he thought it was time to find out who the bugle snatcher was. Tiptoeing forward, Bert and Charlie grasped the stone and managed to roll it back. Sure enough, it had covered a large hole—in which, crouched together, were Danny Rugg and Jack Westley!

And in Jack's hand was Charlie's missing bugle!

"Give me that!" Charlie cried furiously and grabbed away his instrument.

At once Danny and Jack leaped from the hole and tackled the two other boys, who were somewhat smaller. The bugle flew out of Charlie's hand and, luckily, landed in some sod off to the side.

Charlie sent a hard blow to Jack's cheek.

This infuriated the bully, and he gave Charlie a punch in the chest.

Meanwhile, Bert was having a tussle with Danny. The heavier boy had him pinned on the ground, but suddenly Bert rolled him over.

"You smashed my walkie-talkie," Bert panted accusingly. "And then knocked me out!"

Danny did not reply. In a second they had changed places and Danny was on top, swinging his arms left and right toward Bert's chin.

"I didn't take Charlie's bugle and you can't say I did!" Danny shouted, his face red with anger. "Who do you think you are, anyway? But I'm glad I broke your walkie-talkie, and your head, too!"

Bert was doing his best to defend himself, but found it hard going against the larger boy. He hardly cared, though, for he had had a confession from Danny!

With all his might, Bert gave a sudden upward thrust to his body and knocked Danny off balance. They rolled over once more, with Bert now on top of the bully. He caught a momentary glimpse of the other two wrestlers. At this point Charlie was sitting on Jack!

The fight might have gone on, with neither side winning, except that suddenly a voice cried, "What's going on here?"

The four boys looked up. Allen Shelby stood

before them. The young man had a very commanding look when he was angry. Danny and Jack at once got to their feet.

"We—we were just having some fun," said Jack lamely.

Charlie ran over to pick up his prize bugle. Waving it in the air, he exclaimed. "We found it!"

Allen looked at the instrument in amazement. He was about to ask for more details when Danny and Jack began to sneak away. "Hold on there!" he said sternly.

The two larger boys stopped in their tracks. Allen now asked Bert and Charlie what had caused the fight. Upon hearing the story, he said to Danny, "Suppose we hear your side."

"All right," the bully answered sullenly. "I didn't take the bugle. But I did come to Bert's house to find out about the bike trip. I was behind the tree when he was using the walkie-talkie and when I heard him tell Charlie I took the bugle, I saw red!"

The boy glowered at Bert. "Nobody can accuse me of something I didn't do, so I gave him a punch. I didn't mean to knock him out." All this time Jack had been standing by silently. But upon receiving a very black look from Danny, he spoke up.

"Some of it's my fault," he said. "When

Danny and I and some other fellows were camping, we saw Charlie with his bugle. We decided to play a joke on him.

"So I—I took his bugle and hid it in this hollow tree. I was going to give it back to him later, honest! But I forgot which tree I put it in."

"Yes, go on," said Allen, as the bully paused.

Again Jack looked toward Danny, who was still scowling at him. "Danny and I came back here to look, but we couldn't find it," he went on. "So we followed Bert and Charlie, to see if they'd located the bugle. Then I remembered where it was, so I took the bugle before Charlie had a chance to."

"We knew about the dirt hole with the stone on top from our other trip here," Danny spoke up. "So we decided to hide there."

"If you were going to return the bugle to Charlie," Bert said, "why did you take it from the tree just now and then try to hide from us?"

"Because I didn't want you to find it here," Jack said. "I was going to leave it at your house." And Bert and Charlie knew he was furious at being outsmarted at his own game.

"Now can we go?" Danny asked Allen.

"Just a moment," said the young man.

Allen shot the question directly at Danny and

Jack. "What did you do with all our food?"

Danny and his friend looked genuinely surprised. The others felt sure that the two knew nothing about the missing food.

"We didn't take it, honest," said Jack.

"I believe you," said Allen. "But can you give us any clues as to who might have?"

The two boys looked at each other, then Danny said, "There's a grouchy old man in these woods. I don't know his name, but he chases everybody away. We saw him pushing a red wheelbarrow in from the main road. It was loaded with stuff."

"When was this?" Bert asked quickly.

"This morning," Danny replied. "Now can we go?"

"All right," Allen told him. "But I'd advise you boys to stop playing jokes that make trouble for other people."

The boys did not reply to his advice, but ran off quickly. After they had gone, the others looked at one another and laughed.

"I'm certainly glad you found the bugle," Allen said. "And it doesn't seem to have been damaged."

Charlie looked his instrument over and declared that it was all right. Then talk turned to the stolen food. They were pretty sure the

Charlie played his serenade again

"grouchy old man" Danny told them about was Jed Rustum. If so, had he really taken their supplies?

"Let's find him," Charlie suggested.

"But we haven't the least idea where he lives," said Allen.

During the past few moments Bert had been staring into space. Now he grinned.

"I think I know a good way to find Jed Rustum," he said.

"How?" Charlie asked.

"Blow your bugle long and loud. I'll bet anything Mr. Rustum'll come running."

"I'll do it."

Charlie set the bugle to his lips and sounded several long-drawn out notes. He repeated these at intervals. As the echoes faded, the trio waited eagerly. But complete silence was the only response.

A few moments later Charlie played his serenade again. This time he had hardly stopped when the boys heard crashing through the bushes not far away. Looking back, the three beheld a red wheelbarrow coming directly toward them. And it was being pushed by an irate Jed Rustum!

CHAPTER XVIII

THE LEAN-TO

WHEN Jed Rustum, red-faced and out of breath, pulled up in front of Bert, Charlie, and Allen, he gazed angrily at them and the bugle.

"Well!" the man shouted. "It's not bad enough that you come pokin' around these woods, but you have to blow *that* thing!"

The others did not answer him. Instead, they were staring at his wheelbarrow. Then Allen said, "We understand that someone with a red wheelbarrow took our food."

For a long moment the two men looked each other straight in the eye. Finally, Rustum lowered his gaze and scraped his foot nervously in the dirt.

"Well, I don't know how you found out," he muttered. "But I did take it."

As the others started to speak, he held up his hand for silence. "Wait! I think I had a right to. You got no business coming in here, breaking down bushes and trees."

Allen and the boys stared at Rustum in astonishment, then stoutly denied that they had broken down anything. Bert told him that there were other boys camping in the woods. Perhaps they had done it.

"Well, maybe so," Rustum conceded. Suddenly the angry look left his eyes. The old man looked almost pathetic as he went on, "I love Beechcroft Hill. I've lived here for nearly fifty years. I just hate to see the place spoiled. I thought sure you had done it, and figured maybe if you didn't have any food to eat, you'd move off. So when you were away from that cave, I sneaked in and took your eats."

The caretaker promised to bring back what he had taken. "On one condition though," he added, with a half-smile, "that you won't blow that confounded bugle!"

Charlie promised, and the old man went off to get their food. Bert and his friends went directly back to the cave. Jane, the younger girls, and Freddie were overjoyed to see the bugle, and demanded the full story at once.

"I hope the other three mysteries will be solved as soon as yours was, Charlie," Nan said.

"And it's very 'portant to find Snowball," Flossie remarked. "It's more'n a week since she got lost."

"But the fire-bomb is important, too," Freddie insisted.

Nan smiled. "And don't forget poor Mrs. Elliott. She and Susan can't have their new home unless we find her missing money."

In a little while Jed Rustum returned, trundling his red wheelbarrow. In it were piled the campers' food supplies. "Well," he said, pleasantly for him, "eat hearty."

The girls served a tasty supper which they had hardly finished eating when the wind began to blow hard. Jane, who was clearing up, looked at the sky, a bit worried.

"I'm afraid it's going to rain," she said.

"Maybe it will blow over," Allen said hopefully.

But the wind did not abate. It grew in intensity, and Bert was unable to contact his father on the walkie-talkie. Finally the Shelbys decided that they had better build a large lean-to.

Each of the children helped. The Bobbseys had often made these while on camping trips and knew just how to go about it. First they found a row of trees on a level spot so water would not run down into it.

Next they gathered branches that were covered with leaves and lashed them tightly to the trees at a forty-five degree angle. When this backing was on, the campers took their ponchos and laid them across the boughs.

The shelter was barely completed when it began to rain very hard. The group huddled under the lean-to. How good it felt to get away from the wind and the heavy downpour!

"I hope it won't last long," said Jane. "This kind of a lean-to is all right for a while, but I'd hate to have to stay under it all night."

She had barely spoken when there was a vivid streak of lightning, followed by a loud thunderclap. Flossie huddled against Nan. She was not frightened, but the sharp flashes and the rumbling thunder made her ears and eyes hurt.

At that moment, it began to pour harder than ever, the wind driving the rain into the lean-to. The campers moved back as far as they could into the shelter, but still they were getting wet.

Suddenly they heard a voice calling, "Hal-lo!"

"Do you suppose somebody's looking for us?" Nan asked in surprise.

Again the voice called, "Hal-lo! Where are you?"

Bert peered outside. Off at a little distance stood Jed Rustum.

"My goodness, you folks must be 'most drowned!" he said. "You come up to my cabin right away."

Jed Rustum really seemed like a different

man! As he repeated his invitation, Jane and Allen exchanged glances. They nodded to each other.

"Thank you very much," said Jane. "We'll be glad to come. We really are drenched."

Clutching their ponchos tightly about them, the group followed the elderly man through the woods. Water swashed into their hiking shoes and the rain was coming down so hard they could hardly see where they were going. But soon they came to a log cabin. It stood in a small clearing, and near it was a barn.

Jed Rustum pushed open the cabin door and the others trooped in. The place had three rooms—a large living room where an open fire was roaring, a bedroom, and a kitchen. How good the fire felt! The campers removed their shoes and set them to dry in front of the blaze.

"I guess you're all chilled clean through," said Mr. Rustum. "How about some soup to warm you up?"

All his guests nodded vigorously. He went into the kitchen and returned in a few moments with a tray bearing nine bowls of steaming soup. Everyone declared it was wonderfully warming.

Presently, a clock began to strike. Flossie counted, one-two-three-four-five-six-seven-eight. Turning to Bert, she said:

"We didn't walkie-talkie home tonight."

"That's right," said Bert. "I couldn't get through to them because of the storm. And I didn't bring the walkie-talkie with me."

Jane and Allen Shelby said that they felt the Bobbseys should be notified.

"I'll go get the walkie-talkie," Bert offered.

But Jed Rustum would not hear of this. He said the boy most certainly would get lost in the darkness. He himself would go. He had the proper clothing and knew the woods by heart.

"Furthermore," the old man said, "you all are going to stay here overnight." He grinned. "It's the least I can do for taking your food away from you!"

He disappeared out the door, and the others looked at one another. Wasn't it funny, they thought, how some things that seemed bad at first often turned out to be good?

Mr. Rustum returned in a little while with the shortwave set. Bert signaled his father. Mr. Bobbsey had been waiting two hours for a contact. He and Mrs. Bobbsey were delighted to know the group were safely sheltered for the night.

Before going to bed, Jed Rustum announced that the rain had stopped, and led them out to his barn where he had a wonderful collection of saddles.

"These are swell!" exclaimed Bert, examining one that was particularly wide.

Jed Rustum explained that it had belonged to a fat man in the circus. "And the horse he rode was the widest one I've ever seen."

Later, Jed found blankets and the campers curled up on the floor before the fire, soon falling into deep slumber. During the night the wind blew even stronger and by morning had dried out the woods pretty well. After breakfast the campers thanked their host and set out. In order to cover ground more quickly, Jane decided to stay with the girls and Freddie, while Allen went with Bert and Charlie.

"By tonight we will have combed these woods pretty thoroughly," said the young man. "By tomorrow I think we should move on."

"Oh, I hope we find Snowball today," said Flossie. "I'm going to look real hard."

Jane and her group set off. Presently Flossie was sure she had heard a cat meow.

"Kitty, kitty!" she called. "Where are you?"

The meowing seemed to be not far ahead. She ran a little distance, then paused. Nan, a few yards away, saw that Flossie was standing in the center of a weed-covered railroad track. The girl wondered how many years had passed since it was last used.

Then, the next second, her eyes nearly popped out of her head. An old-fashioned handcar was coming down the rails at a good clip. Flossie apparently did not hear it!

"Flossie!" Nan screamed. "Get off the track!"

But the little girl did not move. The handcar was very close now.

CHAPTER XIX

FREDDIE'S FIND

LEAPING like a gazelle, Nan Bobbsey reached the railroad track and grabbed Flossie in her arms. The next second the old handcar whizzed by!

Quickly Jane, Nellie, and Freddie ran forward and crowded around the two girls. Everyone had been dreadfully frightened, and it was several moments before anyone could speak. Then Nellie said, "Did you see who was on that handcar?"

"No," Nan and Flossie answered together.

"Danny Rugg and Jack Westley," Nellie told them.

"What?" Nan cried.

Jane Shelby said she knew the railroad had not been used for years and years. The boys must have found the handcar and helped themselves to it.

"I've never seen such boys in my life," Jane declared. "It seems as if we can't turn around without those two causing us trouble."

By the time they all moved on, Flossie had gotten over her fright. She listened carefully for any more meows. But none came.

"That handsome car scared Snowball away," she said in disappointment.

Nan smiled at her little sister's funny name for the handcar and reminded her that if Snowball were around she would certainly recognize her family and come to them. Flossie called and called, but the Bobbsey cat did not appear.

"I guess the cat who meowed before was from one of the farms," said Jane finally. "After this, Flossie dear, you'd better not run off alone."

The little girl promised, and the group stayed close together. They inspected the tall grass very carefully, but the lost fire extinguisher was not in sight nor were any of the five-hundred-dollar bills, and there was still no Snowball.

Presently Freddie grew tired of looking. "Jane," he said, "let's go find that handcar and take a ride on it."

The young woman realized that the children had been very faithful to their task and ought to have some time for play.

"All right," Jane said. "I'm not promising that we will use it, because I don't know if we can find the handcar. But at least we'll look for it."

She and the others went back to the railroad tracks and started walking along. They wondered just how far Danny and Jack might have taken the handcar. Perhaps, realizing that there had almost been an accident, the boys might have given up running it.

As they trudged on, hunting for the handcar, Nan said, "There's Bert, Charlie, and Allen up ahead." She began to laugh. "I bet they have the same idea we do."

Nan's statement proved to be true. From another part of the woods Bert and his friends had seen Danny and Jack operating the car.

The bullies had abandoned the car not far away. So the Bobbseys and their friends climbed aboard and off they went.

"This is super-duper!" cried Freddie. "Please, Allen, can I hold the bar?"

The young man let the small boy help pump the handcar for a while, then Bert and Charlie ran it.

"Now we'd better take this back to where Jack and Danny left it," said Allen. As they whizzed back along the track Flossie said:

"This is very 'citing! I wish we owned a handsome car so we could go riding on a railroad any time we wanted."

After the handcar reached the spot where it had been abandoned, everyone climbed off and the search was under way again.

It was not long before they came to an open meadow. Allen consulted his map and said that they must be on the farm which adjoined Beechcroft Hill.

"Which way is it to the cave where we left our bicycles?" Bert asked.

Allen pointed. At once Freddie began to run. "I'll beat you all there," he said gaily.

The little boy had not gone a hundred feet when suddenly he vanished!

"My goodness!" Jane exclaimed. "Where did he go?"

The whole group dashed forward. In a few moments they came to the place where Freddie had disappeared.

He had fallen into a ditch!

How relieved everyone felt! Freddie was not hurt. In fact, he was hurrying along the bottom of the ditch. He paid no attention to the onlookers above him. Instead, the little boy began running very fast, and seconds later he cried out:

"I've found it! The fire extinguisher! I've really found it!"

Excitedly the others slid down the side of the ditch to where Freddie was standing. Lying there was a small glass ball. It *was* Mr. Becker's missing fire-bomb—all in one piece.

"Oh, Freddie, you're wonderful!" his twin cried, hugging him.

The little boy felt very proud. He carefully picked up the extinguisher and studied it.

"Now," he said, "Mr. Becker will make me that toy extinguisher that'll really put out fires!"

The others were very pleased that Freddie had accomplished what he had set out to do on the bicycle trip. They all congratulated him, and the older boys offered to carry the extinguisher. But Freddie would not accept any help.

"I guess if I'm old enough to find it, I'm old enough to carry it," he said.

Freddie wanted to go right home and give Mr. Becker his extinguisher.

"What? And give up the rest of our trip?" Flossie cried, wide-eyed. "We have to find Snowball!"

"Oh, that's right," said Freddie. In the excitement of his discovery, he had momentarily forgotten.

But the little boy's find posed a problem. The extinguisher was too dangerous to be carried on the rest of the bicycle trip.

Bert suggested he use the walkie-talkie to ask his father or Sam to come out and get it.

"I have a better idea," said Nan. "Why don't we take the fire-bomb to Jed Rustum? He can keep it safe for us until we pick it up on our way back home."

The others agreed that this was a good plan. After lunch, they set off across the field toward the log cabin, Freddie proudly carrying the extinguisher.

Soon the hikers came in sight of the cabin. They called Mr. Rustum, but the old man did not answer. Apparently he was not at home.

"We can leave it with a note," said Nan.

As the group moved closer, Freddie suddenly cried: "I see smoke! It's coming from Mr. Rustum's barn! We'll have to use Mr. Becker's fire-bomb! I hope he won't mind."

The small twin was right. Smoke was curling from the roof of the barn!

"Oh dear," Nan gasped, "all his beautiful saddles will be burned up!"

Running like mad, the Bobbseys and their friends covered the rest of the distance to the barn in a short time.

"Now we'll see if this new fire extinguisher does the trick," said Allen, taking it from Freddie. "Everybody stand back."

With a mighty heave, he pitched the fire-bomb through the open door of the burning barn!

CHAPTER XX

A NICE REWARD

BREATHLESSLY, the Bobbseys and their friends waited to see if the fire-bomb Allen had thrown into the burning barn would quench the blaze. For a few seconds nothing happened, then came a great explosion!

"Wow! It's working!" Freddie yelled excitedly.

Within a minute a huge cloud of smoke burst out the barn door. This was followed by tremendous puffs of steam.

"Oh, the fire is worse!" Flossie cried in disappointment.

"Maybe not," said Nan, putting her arms around her small sister. "Mr. Becker never told us exactly how his bomb works."

The smoke and steam continued to pour out for a couple of minutes, then, as if by magic, they suddenly stopped. The onlookers ran forward and poked their heads cautiously inside the old building. To everyone's amazement, there was not a trace of fire nor smoke.

"This is wonderful!" Jane Shelby exclaimed.

"It's pure magic!" said Allen. "I never saw a fire go out so fast in my life!"

Just then old Jed Rustum came hurrying through the woods. From a distance he had smelled smoke and followed its direction. Sure that a campfire was the cause, he was amazed to see the bicycle group standing near his barn.

Freddie spied him first and ran up to the old man. "It works! We put out your fire!"

Jed Rustum stared at the little boy, then asked for an explanation. More slowly Freddie told him exactly what had happened and the man's eyes widened in amazement. Wrinkling his forehead, he shook his head and said, "I think the fire was all my fault, too."

With that, he ran inside and the others exchanged puzzled looks. But when Mr. Rustum reappeared, he announced that the blaze had started on the very bench where he had left his lighted pipe. He thanked the campers over and over for having saved the building and his fine collection of old saddles.

The elderly man smiled. "It's mighty lucky for me that I made friends with you folks after all. I'd like to give you some kind of reward."

He led the way into his cabin and pulled a small stepladder to the center of his living room. In the ceiling was a concealed trapdoor.

"I keep my valuables in the attic," Mr. Rustum explained, chuckling. He mounted the ladder and lifted himself up through the opening.

The children heard bumping and thumping sounds as if trunks were being moved about. Then the old man came to the opening and called down, "Catch these, folks!"

He dropped oddly wrapped bundles into their

arms. Then letting himself down nimbly, he said:

"I came of a large family. When my brothers and sisters and I were kids, we used to dress up in these costumes. I'd like you children to have them."

The children excitedly opened the packages. Flossie chose a little Bo Peep costume and Freddie a clown suit. For Nan and Nellie there were Colonial ladies' dresses. Charlie and Bert put on Minutemen suits of the Revolutionary period. They shaded their eyes and peered out of the window as if an enemy were coming.

All this time Bert was making up a few lines of poetry to recite. Presently he stopped in the

center of the floor and faced Jed Rustum and the others. Striking a pose as if he were firing a rifle, he said:

"I'm a minuteman of Beechcroft Hill,
  I'm ready for a fight.
If any bully comes around,
  I'll fix him day or night!"

The others laughed and Nan called out, "Danny Rugg, beware!"

Jane Shelby said it was time for the bicyclists to be on their way. They said good-by to Jed Rustum, who thanked them once more for saving his barn. He invited them to come again soon to see him. His visitors said they would.

The searchers went back to their camp site for the night, and Bert sent his walkie-talkie message to Mr. Bobbsey. His father was amazed to hear the latest news.

"Mr. Becker will certainly be relieved to know that you found his extinguisher," Mr. Bobbsey remarked. "And he'll be happy to hear that it was put to such good use."

Early the next morning the group had breakfast and packed up to continue their trip.

"What's our next stop?" Allen asked the Bobbseys.

"I think it ought to be the woods where Mrs. Elliott stopped for a picnic," Nan spoke up. "She may have lost her money there."

The Shelbys thought this was a good plan. All this time Freddie and Flossie had been whispering, and they now asked the young woman if they might wear the costumes Jed Rustum had given them.

"I suppose it will be all right," said Jane. "But I'll pin up your skirt, Flossie. And Freddie, remember to push up the legs on your clown pants before you climb on your bicycle."

The small twins wanted all the others to wear their costumes, too, but it was decided that Nan's and Nellie's skirts were too long and too full. They might catch in the wheels. But Bert and Charlie would put on their minutemen costumes.

The bicyclists started off. What a strange-looking combination they were, dressed in both modern and old-fashioned clothes! Every once in a while a car passed them and the passengers would wave and smile.

Just before noontime, the cyclists came to a small town. The first house they approached had a lovely garden of flowers. As the bicyclists slowed to look at them, the door of the house suddenly opened and a stout woman came hurrying toward the road. She held up her hand and cried out:

"Stop! You're the very children we're looking for!"

CHAPTER XXI

EXCITING NEWS

THE BICYCLISTS stopped short. They gazed in astonishment at the woman who had said they were the very children she was looking for. What did she mean? Was their trip to be stopped?

But now the woman smiled, saying, "I must have startled you, but I was so excited at seeing you that I didn't realize what I was saying. My name is Mrs. Parker."

She went on to explain that a friend of hers had seen the children in colonial costume riding along the road a little while before. The friend had telephoned to Mrs. Parker, saying that perhaps she could stop them and talk to them about a parade.

"A parade?" Freddie spoke up. He loved parades.

"Yes," said Mrs. Parker. "Our little town of Madison is two hundred years old today. That was when the first settlers stopped here. We're having a celebration all week, but the big parade will take place this afternoon."

Mrs. Parker went on to say that there had been bad luck in connection with one of the important floats on which several children were to ride. They were to have been in colonial costume, but some puppies had gotten hold of the suits and dresses and torn them to shreds.

"Of course, it's too late now to hunt for more costumes," the woman said.

"Would you like to borrow ours?" Nan asked.

"Oh, no," Mrs. Parker replied. "Another bit of bad luck is that almost all those children who were to be on the float have come down with the measles!"

"That's a shame!" Nellie exclaimed.

"What I was thinking," said Mrs. Parker, "is that you boys in colonial costume and Little Bo Peep might take the places of the others on the float. The parade will start directly after lunch."

The travelers were startled, but delighted, at the surprise invitation, and after thinking it over, decided it would be grand fun.

Flossie was the first one to speak up. "My sister Nan and her friend Nellie have colonial costumes, too."

"Oh, really?" said Mrs. Parker. "What kind are they?"

Upon hearing that they were colonial dames' dresses, she said, "Perfect! Of course I'd like you girls to be in the parade, too."

Up to this time Freddie had been very quiet. The little boy was fighting to keep back tears. He was the only one who had not been asked to ride in the parade. Finally, with a little sob in his voice, he said:

"Didn't they have clowns in olden times?"

His wistful expression and sad tone touched Mrs. Parker. She walked toward the little boy and put an arm around his shoulders.

"Why, of course they had clowns in olden times," she said. "I'm sorry I didn't remember, and we'd love to have you in the parade."

Freddie's tears changed from sad to happy ones. He wiped his eyes and declared he would be the best clown in all the world while he was riding on the float.

Nan had turned to speak to Jane and Allen Shelby, asking permission for the children to be in the parade. The two young people thought it would be very nice and asked Mrs. Parker if the paraders should dress at her house.

"Yes, indeed," she replied. "Please come in right now. I'd like you to have dinner with me before the parade."

Before sitting down at the table, Mrs. Parker

suggested that the children change back into
their shorts. While they were eating she would
have a woman who worked for her press and
freshen up their costumes for the big parade.

Then Mrs. Parker served her visitors a fine
big meal of fried chicken, lima beans and corn,
with apple pie for dessert.

During the meal Freddie and Flossie told
Mrs. Parker that they were quite used to parades. They had once ridden in a Cinderella
coach.

"How exciting!" she said, smiling.

"That was when we solved the mystery of
the Horseshoe Riddle," Flossie added.

"My, you children have had lots of adventures," Mrs. Parker remarked in surprise.
"Well, since you've been in parades before,
you'll know exactly what to do this afternoon."

At one o'clock the children were shown to
the rooms where they would change their
clothes.

In the room where Bert and Charlie were
dressing, they were having a little trouble with
Freddie. The small boy insisted on putting a
pillow inside his clown suit to make him look
fatter. After he was ready, Freddie had decided to do a somersault. The next moment
one of the seams on his costume burst open!

"Ooo, now I've done it!" Freddie cried, worried. "Maybe I can't be in the parade after all."

Bert went for Mrs. Parker. She laughed, came in with her sewing basket, and in a few moments she had the clown suit fixed.

"Please do stay in one piece!" she begged, chuckling.

The children and the Shelbys followed her outdoors to a station wagon. She drove into the center of town where flags and bunting were flying. The streets looked very colorful and gay, and in the distance the children could hear a band playing.

"Isn't this 'citing?" Flossie asked.

"Yes, it is," said Nan, smiling at her small sister.

In a few minutes they reached the float on which the children were to stand. At the back of it was a little fort, and standing against it were two rifles which Mrs. Parker said Bert and Charlie were to hold over their shoulders. The "minutemen" climbed up and took their positions.

Nan and Nellie were told to sit in rocking chairs at the front end of the float. Flossie was to stand alongside Nan.

"Now we'll have to decide where to put you, Freddie," said Mrs. Parker.

The little boy looked the float over and asked

if he might be right in the center of it. "Then once in a while I can do a trick," he said.

"All right," Mrs. Parker agreed. "Climb up, then."

Pretty soon the parade got under way. The band marched along first, playing a lively tune. Everyone lining the sidewalks of the main street waved and shouted. As the float carrying the Bobbseys and their friends came by, there was loud hand clapping.

"Those youngsters have certainly caught the spirit of the celebration!" remarked a man to his wife.

Bert and Charlie stood motionless, and Nan and Nellie, busy with some knitting, merely looked up and smiled. But Flossie kept on waving to the crowd, while Freddie did somersaults, as well as his trick of pulling the stick out of his sleeve and making it disappear.

"Those children are putting on a wonderful show!" exclaimed Mrs. Parker, who was seated in the grandstand next to Jane and Allen. They all waved and clapped as the float went by.

Not long afterward the parade was halted. A woman on the curb began to talk to the small Bobbsey twins. Flossie, in turn, began to tell her about the bicycle trip which they were making.

"We're hunting for lost things," she said.

"We've found two of them. But we still have to find the money for the little house and a pussycat, too."

The woman looked very interested. "Money?" she said. "Are you by any chance looking for a roll of big bills?"

All the children on the float were startled and together answered, "Yes! Five-hundred-dollar bills."

The woman smiled. "Then I guess your worries are over," she said. "I've found them!"

CHAPTER XXII

A YOUNG PHOTOGRAPHER

"WHERE are the five-hundred-dollar bills?" Freddie eagerly asked the woman who claimed she had found them.

At this moment the parade started off again. The woman called after the children, "I live at 212 Main Street. Come to my house after the parade."

As the float moved along, the Bobbsey twins almost forgot to play their parts.

"Aren't we lucky?" Flossie whispered to Nan, squeezing her hand.

"Yes, we are," replied her older sister.

Soon the parade ended. Immediately Nan asked a girl standing on the sidewalk the way to 212 Main Street. The girl pointed and the Bobbseys and their friends hurried off.

When they reached the house, a sign on the lawn read: RAMSEY.

"Maybe Mrs. Ramsey isn't home from the parade yet," Flossie said, worried.

Nan rang the bell. In a few moments the

woman they had met opened the front door.

"Come in," she invited them cordially, and added as they stepped into her living room, "My, how nice you children look! And you played your parts very well."

"Thank you," said Flossie. "And now, may we have the money?"

Nan wished Flossie were not so eager, but Mrs. Ramsey did not seem to mind. She laughed and said she could understand the little girl's impatience. She walked toward a table on which lay a large book.

"I was pressing the bills in this book," she explained. "They were pretty crumpled."

All eyes were turned on the book as Mrs. Ramsey opened it. She turned several pages, but at last found the right one. She reached for the bills and extended them toward Flossie.

It was toy money!

Flossie's face fell and also those of the other children. Mrs. Ramsey, seeing their disappointed looks, was puzzled.

"Isn't this your lost play money?" she asked.

Flossie was so disappointed, tears ran down her cheeks. "But we weren't looking for play money," she said, a catch in her voice.

Now it was Mrs. Ramsey's turn to be surprised. "You don't mean you were looking for real five-hundred-dollar bills?" she asked.

All the children nodded and Nan explained the situation. Mrs. Ramsey said she was dreadfully sorry to have led them all astray. When Flossie had said, "We're looking for money for the little house," the woman had thought she meant play money, of course. Only the day before she had found the wad of make-believe bills on the main street of Madison.

"It was a natural mistake," Bert spoke up.

"Yes," said Nan, "and this means we'll have to look all the harder."

The children hurried from the house and went directly to where Mrs. Parker had parked her station wagon. She was waiting for them and they drove to her home, telling the story of their recent disappointment over the toy money. Upon reaching her house, the children changed to their bicycling clothes while Jane and Allen attended to stocking up with fresh food.

When they were ready to leave, Mrs. Parker thanked them again for being in the parade. All of them declared it had been a lot of fun.

That evening they found a pleasant camp site near Mrs. Elliott's picnic spot and Bert sent his nightly walkie-talkie message to Mr. Bobbsey. He laughed heartily at the story of the toy money and wished them luck in finding the real bills.

After supper Nellie brought out all the pictures she had taken of their adventures. She had a good many of them and Jane Shelby declared it was a wonderful record of the trip.

"Oh, here I am in the ditch finding the fire extinguisher," said Freddie, who had not realized Nellie had taken his picture then.

"And here's one of me pumping the handcar!" said Bert.

Soon it became dark and the bicyclists climbed into their sleeping bags. Everyone slept soundly but was awake early the next morning. While Freddie was waiting for breakfast to be cooked, he became interested in a playful chipmunk.

"I'd like to take his picture," thought Freddie.

Nellie was not around and her camera was lying on top of her sleeping bag. The little boy picked it up and looked it over.

Freddie, several times, had watched Nellie take pictures with the wonderful camera and he tried to remember how she had done it. Knowing that he had to open it and pull out the lens, Freddie pushed a button. Nothing happened! He tried another. Suddenly the back of the camera popped open!

"Oh dear!" Freddie thought. "I hope I haven't broken it!"

At this moment Nellie came up. Seeing the little boy with the open camera, she cried, "Oh, Freddie, what have you done?"

Freddie explained, asking fearfully if he had ruined the camera. Nellie said no, not the camera, but he had opened the back instead of the front lens part. The film would be light-struck.

"I was only trying to take a picture of a chipmunk," said Freddie.

"Never mind," Nellie replied. "I have another film and I'll put it in and take a picture of the chipmunk for you."

She did this and then the two went to have breakfast. When Nellie removed the picture from the camera to show the others, it was a very good one of the little chipmunk sitting on a branch of a tree, cracking a nut.

"Here, Freddie, you may have it," she said.

"Oh, thank you," said the little boy and put the picture into his pocket. "I think when I grow up I'll be a photographer."

The other Bobbseys laughed. Every so often, Freddie decided that he was going to undertake a different kind of work when he grew up. In turn, he had wanted to be a fireman, a policeman, a detective, a train conductor, and many other things. Now he was going to be a photographer!

As soon as breakfast was over, the group began a new search for the missing money and for Snowball. Spreading out in a line, they carefully looked over every inch of ground as they went along. But in these woods, all they seemed to see were empty soda bottles and discarded cans.

"This is an ideal picnic spot," said Jane. "But why do people have to leave things like this around to spoil the landscape?"

"I'll bet it's not children," Freddie spoke up. "We learn in school never to throw bottles or cans and papers on the ground after we've had a picnic."

Nan smiled. "And we learn it from our parents, too," she said.

"Well, I wish everyone would learn it," said Jane crossly.

The group walked in silence for some time. Nan had been unusually quiet. She was interested in watching the many, many birds in these woods.

"I wonder why there are more here than in most places," she asked herself.

Presently she thought she had the answer. The woods smelled very sweet. Deciding that there must be flowers near by, the girl began looking for them. Presently, some distance ahead, she saw some unusual-looking lilies.

"Oh, I must see them up close," she thought and hurried ahead of the others. Then, turning back, she called, "Oh, I've just had an idea, everybody. Nellie's picture of the robin carrying things in his beak gave me—"

A horrified shriek from Flossie interrupted Nan's sentence and Freddie yelled, "Watch out!"

Nan looked around. Almost directly ahead of her was a large billygoat.

"Oh!" she gasped, wondering if the animal were friendly or fierce.

Just then the billygoat charged toward her, his horns lowered!

CHAPTER XXIII

NAN'S WONDERFUL IDEA

FOR A second Nan Bobbsey was almost petrified with fright as the big goat charged toward her. But instantly she remembered Bert's experience at Uncle Daniel's farm. She must not let him toss her into the air!

Nimbly, the girl jumped out of the goat's path. But the old fellow stopped short, turned, and charged at her again!

Flossie and Freddie were shrieking. Their cries seemed to anger the animal more than ever. Allen, Bert, and Charlie started to dash forward. But they were too far away to do any good.

Nan watched her chance. She had decided to try playing a trick on the billygoat. She stood in front of a large maple tree and just before the goat reached her, she jumped aside.

Wham! the goat ran full tilt into the tree, burying his horns in it!

"Oh!" Flossie cried. She was relieved but knew that the danger was not yet over.

The goat struggled to free himself. He twisted and yanked, pawing the ground furiously. By this time the boys had reached him and held him tightly, not permitting the animal to get his horns from the tree. But the old billy was very strong, and they were not sure how long they could hold him.

"Help! Help!" Nellie cried out.

"Help! Help!" Flossie and Freddie screamed at the top of their lungs.

A few seconds later they heard crashing through the underbrush and a farmer appeared. In his hand he held a rope, a collar, and a muzzle. He dashed up to the goat, which was still a prisoner.

"Thank goodness, this old fellow got stuck!" the man said. "He's a bad one, and I've been trying to catch him for some time."

"How did he get loose?" Allen asked sternly. "We came near having a bad accident here!"

The farmer apologized. As he clasped the collar around the animal's neck and put the muzzle over his nose, the man explained that two boys had been prowling around the farm, causing all kinds of mischief.

"They opened the gate to the pen where I keep this old goat," the farmer explained. "If I ever lay my hands on those boys, I'll—I'll—"

"Who were they?" Bert spoke up.

"I don't know," the man replied, "but one of them called the other Danny."

Upon hearing this, Freddie, who had come up when everything was safe, started to say "Oh, I—"

The others knew that he was going to name Danny Rugg. Quickly Nan whispered to him, "Hush! You mustn't be a tattletale, especially when you're not *sure.*"

Freddie said no more, but he felt that if the two bad boys were Danny and Jack, they ought to be punished. Hadn't they nearly caused his sister Nan to be badly hurt?

When the farmer heard exactly what had happened, he praised Nan for her quick-wittedness. He even laughed a little and said to the goat:

"You're a smart old fellow, but it took a girl to get the better of you!"

Everyone laughed to hear this. Then the man asked them all if they would come up to his house.

"I'm sure Mrs. Farmer would love to give you a picnic lunch," he said.

"Oh, that would be fun," Flossie spoke up.

The Shelbys agreed to the plan and the group followed the man and the goat through the woods. In a few minutes they came to a fine-looking farm. Green pasture land with a brook running through it lay on one side of the large white house. On the other side were fields of corn. Back of the house were two large red barns and alongside one were several pens.

As they reached the pens, the farmer explained that he used to keep several goats here. Now the only one he had left was the old billy.

The man went inside the nearest pen, and the boys noticed that he tied up the runaway. Apparently he was going to keep him very still for a while so that he would forget all ideas of breaking loose.

"Now I'll introduce you to Mrs. Farmer," the man said.

Flossie ran forward and took hold of his hand. "What's your wife's real name?" she asked.

The man smiled. "It's Mrs. Farmer," he replied.

"I mean," said the little girl, "what is her name when she's not a farmer?"

"Oh, Mrs. Farmer is never a farmer," said the man. "She's a music teacher."

Flossie looked at him, completely confused. "She's a farm music teacher?" she asked.

"Well, I guess you might call her that," said the man, "but she doesn't give lessons here. She goes to people's houses and teaches the children."

"But why do you call her a farmer if she's a music teacher?" the little girl persisted.

At this the man laughed loudly. "I guess I've teased you enough," he said, rumpling Flossie's curls. "It sounds strange, but our real name is Farmer. I happen to be a farmer, too, but my wife isn't."

Flossie thought about this a moment, then she smiled. "I think it's nice for a farmer to be called Mr. Farmer," she said. "But I think your wife's name ought to be Mrs. Music."

Everyone laughed and after they were introduced to Mrs. Farmer, they told her what Flossie had said. She laughed, too, and said maybe she should have still another name—Mrs. Cook.

"Let's have our picnic lunch," she said, upon hearing her husband's invitation. "Would you all like to come into the house first and wash your hands and comb your hair? Then, if you'd like to go sit under that big tree where the bench is, I'll bring you some sandwiches and milk."

In a little while she brought out a platter stacked with peanut butter and jelly, lettuce, bacon and tomato, and cheese sandwiches. When the group finished eating, Allen Shelby tried to pay the farmer. But he said he had enjoyed meeting the group and the picnic

lunch was the least he and his wife could do
to make up for giving Nan such a scare with
the old billygoat.

After everyone had rested awhile, the
searchers set off again on their great hunt.
They went back into the woods, and, as before,
spread out in line. Presently Jane called to
Nan:

"What was that great idea you had, Nan,
that you were going to tell us when you were
interrupted by the goat?"

The Bobbsey twin had almost forgotten it.
Now she thought a moment, then replied, "Oh,
I was thinking of Nellie's picture of the robin
carrying things in his beak. I thought maybe
birds might have found Mrs. Elliott's money
and picked the bills up."

"That's very possible," Jane said thoughtfully, and all the others nodded.

"Do you think they carried the bills to their
nests?" Flossie spoke up.

"Yes, I do," said Nan. "Why don't we look
in every single nest we can find?"

This thought gave new excitement to the
search. Immediately every one of the children
started climbing trees. Bert and Charlie chose
the tall ones, while Jane insisted that Freddie
and Flossie stick to the low ones. Allen decided
on one with a very fat trunk and climbed up.

There were nests in a couple of the trees but nothing in them. Down the searchers climbed. But they were not discouraged and each chose another tree and went up again. This procedure went on for some time, with some of the children in the trees, others on the ground choosing other trunks to climb, and some high up, hidden in the branches. There was one disappointment after another as they peered into nests of all sizes.

It became very quiet in the woods as the search went on. Then suddenly the stillness was broken by a shout from Nan.

"Come here, everybody, quick!" she cried out.

CHAPTER XXIV

TWO FRIGHTENED BULLIES

AS THE others quickly climbed down the trees and came running toward Nan, the girl scrambled down the trunk. In her hand she clutched a five-hundred-dollar bill!

"Is it real? Honest-to-goodness real?" Freddie asked excitedly, jumping up and down.

Nan handed the bill to Allen Shelby. After examining it closely, he declared it was good United States money.

"Your hunch was right, Nan," Allen said admiringly. "Birds did carry off Mrs. Elliott's money."

Now a frantic search began for the other five bills which Mrs. Elliott had lost. The twins, Nellie, Charlie, and the Shelbys scampered up and down one tree after another like monkeys.

They looked not only for whole bills but pieces of them, in case the birds had pecked them apart to line their nests.

An hour later, Jane called a halt. Everyone

In her hand Nan clutched a five-hundred-dollar bill!

was tired and discouraged. There had not been a single sign of any of the other bills.

"I think if we have an early supper," she said, "then we might go on and do some more searching before dark."

The group trudged back to their camp site and opened some cans of meat. Nan toasted slices of bread and Nellie prepared soup on the little folding stove. This, together with canned fruit, made a very substantial meal. After eating, everyone felt refreshed and was eager to start again on the hunt.

"There's no necessity of going far away," said Jane. "Plenty of trees around here have nests in them, I'm sure."

The searchers were, in a short time, scrambling again up tree trunks and along branches. It was not long before Nan Bobbsey found two more five-hundred-dollar bills, carefully tucked in a robin's nest!

"Even if we don't find any more money," she said happily, "at least Mrs. Elliott will have fifteen hundred dollars toward her new home."

But the campers' luck continued. Nellie found one bill, Jane another, and Allen the last of all.

"Hurray! Hurray!" Freddie shouted, coming down the young maple he had climbed.

"What time is it?" Nan asked suddenly.

Jane Shelby looked at her wrist watch and said that it was five-thirty.

"Oh, I don't want to wait until six o'clock to use the walkie-talkie," said Nan. "Please, may I run up to the farmer's house and telephone Mrs. Elliott right away?"

Jane agreed and asked Bert and Charlie to go along with her. Nellie said she would like to go, too.

When they reached the farmhouse, the two girls went inside to make the call, but Bert and Charlie walked around outside. Suddenly Bert halted his friend.

"Look over there!" he said, pointing to the goat pens. "I just saw two boys sneaking around the corner. I'm sure they're our old friends."

Charlie grinned. "You mean Danny and Jack?"

Bert nodded and added, "Let's play a joke on them."

"Sure thing," Charlie agreed. "Nothing would suit me better than to get square with those two. What'll we do?"

The boys slipped out of sight of the bullies, who, they were sure, had not seen them. They held a little conference, then decided to give Danny and Jack a good scare.

"Let's toss them into that old billygoat's

pen," Bert chuckled. "The animal's tied, so he can't hurt them. But maybe the boys won't notice that."

Cautiously Bert and Charlie crept forward. Presently they saw Danny and Jack crouching in front of the goat's pen. Danny had his hand on the lock, and Bert and Charlie were sure he meant to release the animal again.

"It's time to jump 'em!" Bert whispered.

He and his friend leaped forward. Bert grabbed Danny, and Charlie took Jack. The two bigger boys, taken off guard, had no chance to defend themselves. They were raised up and tumbled over the fence.

At once there was a scream of fright from Danny, and Jack groaned. As both bullies tried to clamber back over the side of the pen, Bert and Charlie grinned.

"The goat'll charge us!" Danny wailed. "He'll stab us with his horns!"

The goat, aroused by the commotion, yanked at his rope and tried to reach the boys who had been dumped into his pen. But he could not, of course, and suddenly Danny and Jack realized the reason for this.

"Why, you—you—" they sputtered angrily.

Bert and Charlie ran off and scooted back to the farmhouse. They hurried into the kitchen and from a window watched Danny and Jack run away as fast as they could. While they were still chuckling over the joke they had played, Mr. Farmer came into the room. They told him what they had done and he also laughed.

"Good for you!" he said. "I'm sure those mean boys won't come back here again soon."

Nan and Nellie walked into the kitchen just then. Nan said that Mrs. Elliott was overjoyed to learn that her money had been found.

"I should think she would be!" Mr. Farmer remarked. "Maybe I'll start hunting in birds' nests myself. With any luck, I could retire on what I might find hidden in them!"

The jolly group separated and the Bobbsey twins started off for the camp site with Charlie and Nellie. When they reached the others, they found Flossie looking very sad. She complained that everything had been found except her beloved pussycat, Snowball.

"And she's the nicest cat in Lakeport," the little girl told Jane and Allen.

Conversation turned to what the bicyclists had best do next. Certainly there had been no sign of Snowball in these woods. Perhaps they should ride along the road to continue their search for the missing cat.

"Do you know what I think?" Flossie spoke up. "Snowball wouldn't stay in the woods, anyhow."

"Where do you think she'd go?" Allen asked her.

Flossie said she was sure that Snowball would have found a nice barn to stay in. There she would find mice to catch and hay to sleep in and she wouldn't get wet when it rained.

"There's a lot of logic in what you say," Allen told her.

Nan gave her small sister a squeeze. "Flossie," she said, "we'll look in every barn from here to Uncle Daniel's farm!"

This made the little girl very happy and soon after she had crawled into her sleeping bag, she was deep in slumber. In the morning Flossie urged everyone to make an early start. Nevertheless, they took time for a good breakfast before setting off.

The cyclists pedaled along the country road for nearly two miles before coming to a barn. The group stopped and inspected the place thoroughly. They found two cats inside, but neither one was Snowball.

They continued on and during the morning looked through four more barns. There was still no sign, however, of the Bobbseys' missing cat.

"Oh dear!" Flossie sighed. "Think of all the cats we've seen today and not one of them is my Snowball."

Just before twelve o'clock, as Jane was suggesting that they stop for lunch, Flossie spied another barn a little distance ahead. She begged that they search it before eating.

The cyclists dismounted and left their bikes against an embankment. Then they walked up a driveway to the big white barn. Just before they reached it, a beautiful white cat came through the doorway and gazed at them. Flossie could hardly believe her eyes.

"Snowball! Snowball!" she cried, running forward. "We've found you at last!"

To her complete astonishment, Snowball did not come toward her. Instead, the cat turned and dashed back into the barn.

Flossie burst into tears. "Snowball doesn't love us any more!" she cried.

The others were just as surprised as Flossie at the cat's actions.

"Maybe," said Charlie, "Snowball's gone wild. Cats do that sometimes!"

CHAPTER XXV

A GREAT DISCOVERY

AS THE Bobbseys' pet cat ran away from them, everyone was puzzled. Surely Snowball had not gone wild as Charlie had suggested. But why was she avoiding them?

In a moment Nan thought she had the answer. "Maybe Snowball only wants to show us where she's been living," the girl said. "Let's follow her and find out."

The twins and their friends entered the barn. Snowball was not to be seen, but they could hear her meowing up in the loft.

"Let's climb up," Flossie suggested.

She had seen a ladder leading to the loft and now began to ascend. Reaching the top, she walked over to where Snowball was standing. This time the white cat did not run away. Instead, she rubbed against the little girl's legs and began to purr.

"Snowball, what's the matter with you?" Flossie asked, leaning down and stroking her pet.

By now Freddie was standing beside his twin, and a moment later they were joined by all the other children and the Shelbys. Snowball seemed very friendly now, going from one person to another.

"There's some reason why Snowball is acting like this," said Nan.

A moment later Flossie held up her hand and said, "Listen!"

From somewhere deep in the hay they could hear several tiny mews and the little girl exclaimed:

"Those are baby kitten sounds!"

She dashed over to where the sounds were coming from and exclaimed in glee. Before her eyes, nestled in the hay, were four tiny kittens!

Snowball had followed her and now proudly licked each one of her babies. The children crowded around and gasped in astonishment.

"Aren't they adorable?" Nan exclaimed. She laughed. "So this is why Snowball didn't try to find her way either to Lakeport or to Uncle Daniel's farm."

Jane smiled, saying, "Snowball never could have made it with all those babies."

Flossie climbed down the ladder and ran for the cat's basket which was still fastened to her bicycle. Returning with it, she lined it with soft hay, then the cat and her family were put into it.

The little girl did not want anyone else to handle the basket, but Jane insisted upon carrying it down the ladder for her. Then when they reached their bicycles, she made certain that the cat's basket was securely placed in the larger wire basket on Flossie's two-wheeler.

Meanwhile, Allen had walked over to the farmhouse which stood not far from the barn. There he had explained to the farmer's wife that Flossie was sure the white cat in the barn was her own lost Snowball.

The farmer's wife chuckled. "Tell the child to take the cat and her kittens too, and welcome," she said. "We have so many kittens around here that we don't know what to do with them all."

After Allen returned, the long ride homeward began. When six o'clock came, and they found a camping spot for the night, Flossie begged to be the one to speak over the walkie-talkie and tell the good news about Snowball.

"All right," said Bert.

He clicked the walkie-talkie on and off as Flossie spoke with her father. Mr. Bobbsey said that he was more amazed about their finding the cat than he was about the missing articles. He promised to get in touch with Uncle

Daniel immediately and tell him the story.

The bicyclists had to make one more overnight stop before arriving in Lakeport. But at last they reached their town and rode at once to the Bobbsey home. To their amazement, there was a great crowd of people, young and old, in front of the house. As the cyclists came into view, the welcomers began to cheer.

"Hurray! Hurray for the Bobbsey twins!"

"And hurray for Nellie and Charlie, too," cried some of their friends.

"And Jane and Allen Shelby," said Mrs. Bobbsey, smiling.

"Yes," added Mr. Bobbsey. "It was certainly an exciting trip and I'm pleased that everything has turned out so well."

What hugging and kissing there was among the Bobbseys as the children reached the porch! Dinah and Sam stood there, too, grinning and congratulating them. Dinah said, chuckling, "My honey lambs, you did all the things you said you were going to!"

After greetings had been exchanged all around, Mr. Price, the newspaper reporter, and the photographer who had taken the children's picture before the trip pushed their way forward and requested a story.

"Tell us all about your treasure hunt!" the reporter requested.

While the children talked excitedly all at once, a man came running up through the crowd. He was Mr. Becker, the inventor.

"I've come to keep my promise," he said, a broad smile on his face. "Freddie, I never can thank you enough for finding my fire-bomb, and proving how good it is. Here's the toy one that really works."

When the photographer heard the story, he insisted that Freddie pose for a picture with the new toy fire extinguisher. Then he took another one of Flossie with Snowball and her kittens, and finally several of all the Bobbseys and their friends.

Just then Mrs. Elliott and her daughter Susan arrived. The woman wept a little, saying that Nan had done her the most wonderful favor in the world. Now she and Susan could have their little home and the first guest to be invited would be Nan Bobbsey!

The Bobbsey twin blushed at the praise. She unzipped the money pocket in her shorts and handed over the bills which they had discovered in the birds' nests.

"This deserves a special story," declared the reporter, beginning to write notes quickly on his pad.

"And don't forget about my bugle," Charlie said.

Finally he and Nellie said they should be going to their own homes. Jane and Allen Shelby declared that they must say good-by, too. The Bobbseys thanked them over and over for taking the group on the trip.

Jane smiled and said, "We'll never forget our wonderful bicycle trip with the Bobbsey twins and their friends."

"We won't forget either," Flossie spoke up. She and the others wondered for a moment what adventure might happen next, never dreaming it would be about THE BOBBSEY TWINS' OWN LITTLE FERRYBOAT.

"Oh, I'm so-o happy," declared Flossie. She was holding all of Snowball's family on her lap. "The trip was the most helpingest one I ever took."

Everyone laughed, and Mrs. Elliott and Mr. Becker agreed. Even Snowball seemed to agree with what the little girl had said. The pure-white cat nestled happily against Flossie and purred herself to sleep.